Also by Alane Ferguson:

YOUNG ADULT NOVELS

Poison
Overkill
Show Me the Evidence

MIDDLE GRADE NOVELS

Stardust
The Practical Joke War
Cricket and the Crackerjack Kid

PICTURE BOOK

A Tumbleweed Christmas

secrets

ALANE FERGUSON

Simon & Schuster Books for Young Readers

SIMON & SCHUSTER BOOKS FOR YOUNG READERS
An imprint of Simon & Schuster Children's Publishing Division
1230 Avenue of the Americas, New York, New York 10020
Copyright © 1997 by Alane Ferguson
SIMON & SCHUSTER BOOKS FOR YOUNG READERS
is a trademark of Simon & Schuster.
Book design by Paul Zakris
The text for this book is set in 11-point Baskerville Book
Printed and bound in the United States of America
First Edition
10 9 8 7 6 5 4 3 2 1

LIBRARY OF CONGRESS CATALOGING-IN-PUBLICATION DATA
Ferguson, Alane.
  Secrets / by Alane Ferguson. – 1st ed.
        p.   cm.
  Summary: On one of his frequent trips to the zoo, T. J. meets a
woman who turns out to be his biological mother and as he gets to
know her and his sister over the course of the summer, he must
choose between his new-found family and the man who adopted
him twelve years ago.
  ISBN 0-689-80313-3
  [1. Adoption–Fiction. 2. Parent and child–Fiction.
3. Brothers and sisters–Fiction.] I. Title.
PZ7.F3547Se 1997
[Fic]–dc20 96-38782

To Virginia Jones,
a sister by choice

one

"Hey, kid!" the security guard barks. "Do that again, and I'm tossing you out of here!"

For a full second I can't move. I'm holding a brown paper grocery sack, crumpled and stained dark at the top from my sweaty palms.

"Hey—you in the black. I'm talking to you. You hear me?"

"Yeah," I mutter.

The guard stops right in front of me. He's looking me over, up slow and even slower down. It's easy to tell he doesn't like what he sees. The guard is stocky, with a paunch that strains the buttons of his shirt. He's working on a wad of gum like chewing tobacco.

"Wait a second," he drawls, wagging his finger at me. "Your name's T. J., right? I caught you before." He points to a large white sign with red letters that says: FEEDING ANIMALS CAN MAKE THEM SICK.

"Read me that sign, boy."

I'm not saying anything, not moving at all, hoping he'll just give up and move on. I hear the gum snap between his teeth, and then he pushes the whole wad into his cheek with his tongue. "What's the matter—can't you read? Or do you got some kind of mental problem?"

When I won't answer, he snorts like I'm too dumb to talk to. That makes me even madder. Crunching my bag into a ball, I toss it into a nearby trash bin. "There!" I tell him. "It's just fruit, but now it's gone. Okay?"

The guard heaves a sigh and pushes his cap toward the back of his head. "Look, kid—my job says I got to make sure these animals don't get nothing to eat that they're not supposed to. So just watch it. If I catch you again, you're out. And I can make sure you don't come back. Got it?"

With one more snap of his gum, he leaves me, cussing at me softly under his breath. What the guard said has me worried, because getting bounced out of the zoo would be the worst. Now that it's summer I come here almost every day, and the animals know me like they know their own. My dad, Taylor Joseph Lancaster senior, thinks his twelve-year-old son is wasting time. He always says, "T. J., if you're going to make it in this world, you're going to have to quit dreaming about animals. You've got to deal with people." And I'm always thinking, why?

It drives my dad crazy that I like animals better than humans, but that's the way I feel. You can take an animal out of the wild and put it in a cage and it won't be tamed, because a cage can't break its spirit. So I come to the zoo to watch them, to be with them, to learn from them.

Now Rafiki, my favorite monkey, shrills a high note, and I know he's demanding more food.

"Yeah, yeah, I see you," I call out.

Once I'm sure the guard isn't watching, I go to the trash can and fish out my brown paper sack. There's a smear of melted chocolate ice cream on the bottom, so I go to the grass and wipe it off. I know I'm going to keep feeding the animals—the only difference is that I'll have to be more careful. Never in a million years would I feed Rafiki anything that would hurt him, but no one will listen to me because to them I'm just a kid.

July sun beats down on my hair like a burning fist. I'm reaching in my sack, just getting ready to chuck a warm grape, when I hear them.

"Look, Momma, it's the monkey from *The Lion King*."

A little girl's busy tugging on her mom's daisy sundress until it balloons like a flowered parachute. With one hand, the mom tries to smooth her dress while reading the sign that tells about Rafiki. They've stopped too close to me. It always bugs me when there's a whole lot of space and someone stands right next to me anyway.

"Monkey, monkey, monkey!"

I want them to go away. The girl is the whiny kind I hate, the type that dips at the knee when her mom pulls on her. The girl's hair is white-blonde, stiff at the edges where she's pulled sticky hands through. I don't like kids much, and I especially don't like little girls, probably because I don't have a brother or a sister. I don't even have a mother.

My mom is dead, but it sounds worse than it feels. I don't remember her at all. When I look at old pictures of her holding me when I was a tiny baby, I feel like I'm missing something, but not exactly her. Just . . . something. I watch as the mother swings the kid onto her hip. They lurch on down the path, the kid's head bobbing like a balloon on a string.

Suddenly, Rafiki throws back his head and screeches long and loud. With one arm, he hangs from a big, fake, plastic tree limb. He's mad, I know, 'cause I'm not throwing food into his cage and he's a greedy pig. He shrieks again, then puffs out three short grunts.

"Okay, okay, just keep it quiet!" I say, half under my breath. "I don't want to get busted."

I look over my shoulder. Birds, big macaws so bright they

seem neon, sit on branches, their wings clipped so they can't fly. The deer just stare at me, soulful, from behind their chain-link fence. It's quiet. I'm alone.

"Okay, Rafiki. Catch!"

I chuck the last soggy grape. Rafiki's hand shoots out and plucks it right from the air and shoves it into his mouth, and I'm fingering a warm orange slice when out of the corner of my eye I see a new shadow mingling with mine. For a second I freeze, then scrunch up the bag really fast. Please, I'm saying to myself, don't let it be the guard again! I blink hard, squeezing my eyes tight. When I open them, the shadow is still there. Only bigger. When I turn around, a lady in an olive green uniform with a name tag that says Nancy Champion is staring at me, real hard. She's thin, tall and stretched-out looking, kinda like a pulled piece of taffy. Her eyes are brown, same as mine, and she's squinting as she looks at me. Did she see me feed Rafiki? I try to think of a way to dump my sack in the trash bin that's just out of reach, but she's watching every move I make.

"Having fun?" Even though she's tall, her voice is light, almost flutey.

I just shrug.

"I saw what you were doing. Don't worry," she adds quickly, "I'm not going to tell anyone."

"It's just grapes," I say.

"You come to the zoo a lot, don't you? I've seen you around." I nod.

"Almost every day. You're T. J., right?"

My eyebrows shoot halfway up my forehead, but she just laughs again and says, "Don't look so surprised, I asked our security guard. I said, 'Pete, who's that kid who wears black all the time and has a gold earring?' He knew who you were right off."

"Oh. Well, he doesn't like me much."

"I can't imagine anyone not liking you." She smiles, and her eyes crinkle at the edges. "You're twelve, right?"

"Yeah."

"You really like animals, don't you? What are you, a Libra? Were you born in October?"

I nod again.

"What day?"

I don't like people asking me a lot of questions, but I don't want to get this Nancy mad at me. One word from her, and Pete'd toss me right out. So I kind of pull back a little and say, "October thirteenth."

"October thirteenth." And then she says it again, sort of quiet, under her breath. She pauses, like she's not sure about something. Finally, she puts her hand on me, right on my shoulder. I don't like that, because I'm not a touchy type of person. Even though she's a grown-up and can get me into trouble, I shake her hand off. She quickly drops it to her side.

"Well, T. J., it's nice to finally meet you."

It's not what she's saying, but the way she's saying it that's getting me spooked. I try to act like nothing's wrong, but my guts start jumping like there's a kangaroo kicking inside. It's because I can't figure out what she's after, can't understand why she's staring at me like she can see through me to the back of my skin.

"Look," I say, "thanks for being cool about the fruit I gave Rafiki. But, I've got a lot of stuff to do. I gotta go." My backpack with my Rollerblades is propped against the chain-link fence. I'm slinging it over my shoulder when she says, "Out of the whole zoo, I bet you like Rafiki the most. But you like the big cats, too, right?"

It was one of those questions that might not be one, so I don't answer. Just slide my other arm through the strap. Pull it up. Try to get away. But she's still babbling about animals, like we're in on the same conversation, except she's doing all the talking.

"Let's see—yesterday, you started at the lion house, and then you went on to the bird sanctuary. And the day before that, you were . . ." She taps her chin with a thin finger. "You began at the elephant cage, went straight to the llamas, and ended in the snake house. And on Monday, you sat on a bench in front of the seals right before closing time and ate a hot dog with chili on top and a root beer. Am I right? Or"—she takes a long breath through her lips—"was it the seals on Tuesday and the snake house on Monday? Which was it, T. J.?"

"I don't remember," I say. But the truth is, that's exactly where I've been, which can only mean one thing. It means this woman, this Nancy Champion, must have been watching me. And I've never once seen her.

Being spied on gives you a shivery feeling, like a cold bead's gliding down your spine. I don't want her to know that she's scaring me, so I look her right in the eye, as if there's nothing in the whole world I'm afraid of. Maybe she'll get the idea I'm no one to mess with, which isn't true, but I can seem that way if I try.

"Look," I tell her, my voice low, "I don't like people watching me. If you're going to bust me for chucking a few grapes at Rafiki, then do it. If you're not, then I'm outta here."

"No. Wait!" Even though her hair's pulled into a thin little ponytail, she rakes her fingers across the top of her head, pulling up dark strands. She's talking fast now, her eyes darting around as if she's trying to make sure no one else can hear. "Please, don't get angry, T. J. I want to be your friend. It's—important to me. I can't explain. Not yet. Just give me a chance, okay? Please."

Now her gaze has landed right on me. And that is the strangest part of this whole thing. I have never, in my whole life, had anyone look at me the way she's looking at me right this minute. It's like I'm being pulled into her and I'm part of whatever's going on inside her head and she's got me caught, half breathing, waiting.

I swallow the little bit of spit still left in my mouth. "What do you want?"

Her voice is soft again; the edges of her lips curve. "I can't tell you. Not yet. It's a secret. You like secrets, don't you, T. J.?"

Now her hand's back on my shoulder, and this time I don't shake it off.

Sweat is trickling down the side of my cheek. I could wipe it, but I'm scared to move, because if I do, it might break the spell.

"I want to make a deal with you. Don't worry, it's a deal you're going to like. If you come back and see me tomorrow, I'll take you with me when I feed the animals. All the animals love you."

Rafiki starts to scream. I ignore him. Is this woman dangerous? Do I have something she wants? If she's been following me, she might know my dad's got lots of money. But somewhere deep in me I'm not afraid.

"You don't have to answer. But just think, T. J., if you come back you won't have to be on the outside anymore. I can take you with me. It'll be fun." She puts her fingertips lightly on my cheek, so light it might have been a butterfly landing right on my skin, and she says, "Be here tomorrow. I'll be waiting for you. You have to come. Promise me."

And, even though I don't understand any of it, I nod.

I know I will.

two

I turn my Rollerblades up our driveway, gliding over the smooth concrete as though it were ice. We have a gardener, so our flower beds are perfect. Deep red begonias next to snowy white petunias and miniature red and white roses. Red and white, to match the brick of the house and the large white pillars. My wheels hum as I skate onto our walkway. Groundlights have been planted along our sidewalk, like glowing eggs among the flowers, and I need their light to see where to put my feet. It's extra dark because of the thick, winding trees that lead all the way up to our front door.

The canopy of branches means I have to get real close to my house to find out what I need to know. I skate past the last gnarled trunk and stop. Overhead, a light from my dad's bedroom window glares down at me, like a yellow cyclops eye. I feel myself cringe. That light means two things: It's later than I thought, and my dad is home.

Quickly, I unstrap my skates and sling them over my left shoulder. Dad doesn't like me to skate in the house, which, if you ask me, is a stupid rule. We have tile floors that run all the way through, and that tile must be two inches thick. I say to him, "Why would a few rubber wheels hurt this floor? It's stone. Nothing hurts stone." He says, "Because it's my house and I make the rules. Now take off the skates, son, or I'll take them away from you for good." I guess that sort of sums up the way we talk to each other.

I've barely shut our front door when Midget lopes up to give his usual sloppy hello. He's a rottweiler, which means he's about the biggest dog in the world. My dad doesn't like him roaming the house. I let Midget do whatever he wants.

"Hey, pup," I say. The fact is he's almost three years old, but I call him that anyway. Midget gives me a wet kiss and a loopy dog grin. I ruffle the back of his dark fur, then crouch down and kiss his muzzle. He's dripping spit, but I don't care, until he starts rooting around my pocket, leaving wet streaks on my black shorts.

"Knock it off! I get it. You're hungry—I know, I know." With one hand, I hold him back, and with the other I dig out the McDonald's double cheeseburger I bought him. Now he's going wild, trying to get it.

"I fed you before I left. Here, don't eat my fingers, too. Watch it, Midget—I don't want to pull away a bloody stump!"

Now I hold out the burger, and he inhales it before I can blink. One by one, he licks my fingers. I love the feel of his soft mouth on my skin, and when he's done, I give him a bear hug that's so tight he grunts.

"Well, well, well. It's T. J.! So you finally decided to come home!" My dad's upstairs, but his voice barrels all the way down to me, like a car alarm going off.

"Hi, Dad."

"Were you at the zoo again?"

"No," I lie. I know I shouldn't, but I do. I don't want to face the lecture that's sure to come, because my dad's getting rabid about me going there. He thinks watching animals all day makes my brain soft. I don't even want to start it.

"I lost track of time," I call up. "Don't worry about dinner. I grabbed a burger."

I hear him stop at the top of the steps. In a second, I'll know what kind of night it's going to be. See, I can tell even before I've looked at his face. It's the way he goes down our staircase. Lighter steps mean he's too busy with work to spend much time yelling at me. Lumbering thuds mean a bad day, and I'll catch it for breathing. I listen, and tonight, his feet sound heavy. "Drat!" I spit, under my breath. Trouble again. I pull Midget next to me and stand.

"Do—you—know—what—time—it—is?" With every word, a foot crashes down. "It's a question, son, and I expect an answer!"

The weight of my Rollerblades is biting my shoulder, and I picture me slapping them on and blowing out of here in a cloud of smoke. But there's no way. More footsteps, and then a rush of brown leather slippers, bare doughy legs, and the hem of a jade green terry-cloth bathrobe flapping against my father's knees. My dad must have just gotten out of the shower, because I can smell the too-strong scent of Giorgio shampoo.

"Listen, young man," he begins. "It may be summertime so you think you can come and go as you please, but I am still your father. That means you respect me and show up when I tell you. Understand?" As usual, he's stopped one step short of the entry-way floor. My dad is on the short side, maybe five feet seven if he's puffing his chest and rocking forward on the balls of his feet. I'm already catching up to him. Maybe I'll even be taller by next year. I know he thinks about it, because when he's going to yell, he stands on the bottom step, trying to look bigger than he really is.

"It happens to be nine thirty!" he roars. "You've been gone from this house the entire day!"

Nine thirty? That surprises me. All evening I've been skating around, thinking about Nancy Champion. She's haunting me. I turn what she said over and over, wondering at the way she knew me, remembering the little sparks that popped under my skin when she touched my cheek and questioning why I want to go back. When I really think about it, I don't know if I should. I'm tempted by the animals, by being a part of the zoo itself the way she is. But it's more than the zoo. I want to know the secret she talked about. So I spent the day doing what I always do when my brain is cramped; I skate and think, think and skate.

I must have looked startled when I hear how late it is, because my dad backs off a little.

"Okay. Let's calm down and discuss this. Part of your problem is you never know what time it is. Where's your watch?" He's looking at my bare wrist, and then he starts to shake his head, clucking his tongue between his teeth. "You don't have one on. Again. I've given you at least ten different wristwatches, yet you never bother with any of them." A thick finger wags in my line of vision. "Get your eyes off the ground. Come on, son, look at me when I'm talking to you."

I do. I look up, and I'm staring straight at an old man. I was born when he was fifty, so now he's already going gray and soft, like a grandfather instead of a dad. He's not a bad guy. Sometimes I feel guilty that I'm not more of what he wanted. He's in advertising, owns his own company, and I think he wishes he could have ordered his son from a catalogue instead of having one the normal way. He bombed out when he got me.

"Son, you're running wild. Part of it is my fault. With your mother gone, I've . . . well, there's been no one to tell me how to do this job. I've left you alone a lot. You seemed to like it that way, so I thought there was no harm."

"I like to be by myself," I mutter.

"Except now that you've got those blasted wheels, you come

and go just as you please. I never know where you are. You're only twelve, and you're out roaming creation! The world is a dangerous place, T. J."

"I'm all right. I do fine on my own."

"Fine? You don't look like a kid who's fine. Were you fine when you got that earring? I should sue the girl who shot that idiotic stud in your ear. You're underage, for Pete's sake!"

"Leave it alone, Dad," I say. Even to me, I sound tired.

He's close, but he still doesn't touch me. My dad's not the touching kind, either.

"What are we going to do about this? Do you need a nanny to keep track of you–"

My hands shoot up at that. "Okay, okay. Look, I'll for sure wear a watch tomorrow. I'll be home by five." I say what he wants because I need to get this over with. The thing is, I hate watches. They slice your time in little splinters, and they make you feel guilty for just being. I'll never wear one.

I look straight at him. "Are we done? Can I go now?"

My dad sighs. He rubs his chin with his hand. He's staring at me like he doesn't know what planet I'm from, so I decide to end things right there.

"'Night," I say. I reach down and grab Midget by the collar. "Come on, mutt," I say.

My dog's claws make a scraping sound as I pull him across the tile. I want to get away from my dad as fast as possible. Midget's toes splay apart, but I yank harder, and I'm just getting to the stairs when my dad sees something. In a flash he's grabbed my wrist and pulls it right underneath his eyes.

"Hold on!" His voice suddenly shifts to flinty. "What is this?"

He's pointing to an ink smear right below my knuckles. I try to rub it off, but it's too late. Inside, I groan. It's the stamp they give when you walk through the zoo gate. I left my zoo pass in the pocket of my other shorts, so I had to pay to get in today.

"You *were* at that zoo again, weren't you?" he demands. "You *lied* to me!"

When I don't answer, he drops my hand and slaps a fist against his thigh. It makes a muffled sound through the thick terry cloth. He's fired up again. I try to think of a way out, but nothing comes to mind. I'm just blank. Why didn't I think to rub off the mark? Stupid, stupid, stupid!

"How many times do I have to say this? Make friends with humans. I thought you agreed to try."

"It's not that easy. No one likes what I like."

"Because you waste your life in that smelly zoo when you could be goofing off at the pool or going to the movies with other kids. The only times you're not at the zoo, you're playing with Midget or that blasted parrot. You need friends."

"I have friends," I say. "They're just not people."

"It's not normal, son. You've turned into a loner."

I close my eyes. I know what's coming, and there's no way I can stop him from saying it. A breath, and then the awful words.

"What is wrong with you?"

That question makes me so mad my mouth dries up. I hate it. I already know, from watching everyone else, that there's something not quite right when it comes to the way I look at the world. I don't laugh like the rest of them. I don't smile much. It's like, there's a big joke, and everyone's howling, and I don't get it. But I can't stand him saying it out loud.

Now my jaw is starting to work, right in the joint. "I was at the zoo. So what?" My voice is hot. "If I like animals, it's because animals don't try to make me be anything, or do anything. They—they—" I stop. I can't get it straight, because even I don't know why.

"T. J., you have *got* to join the world. Hard work might turn you around. You need a job–"

"I don't need money."

"I'm not talking about money. I'm talking about responsibility, learning to work with humans and collect a paycheck when you're done. When I was your age, I was already selling magazines door to door. I wasn't losing my summer watching baboons." My dad thrusts his face at me, so I have to look at him. His hair is combed straight back, and his pale blue eyes bulge. "Well, no more. Next week, I'm going to see about getting you started on a paper route–"

"I don't want a job. I want to be left alone!" I push past him and run up the stairs to my room, and when I shut the door I try to close out all the words that my dad shoots after me. I'm not like he is, not like anybody, but it doesn't matter. I make sense to me.

First thing tomorrow, when the big metal zoo gates are opened, I'll be there.

three

It's still raining. Water lies in puddles behind the zoo's wrought-iron gate as I peer though the bars, hoping Marsha will hurry and open up. Puddles are everywhere, and so are long, bloated worms, so I'm careful where I put my feet. My Rollerblades have been cleaned and polished. I don't want too many worm bodies getting stuck in the wheels.

I'm breathing through my mouth because the zoo stinks. It's funny how rain can make some places smell clean, but just make the zoo smell worse. All that animal crap and water just don't mix.

The hands on the big zoo clock slide to 9:03. "Come *on*," I say, trying to keep my teeth from chattering.

Finally I hear humming, so I know Marsha's arriving now. As always, she's wearing something bright enough to make you squint. Today, her shirt is a blazing orange and green jungle print with a Bengal tiger leaping right out of its center. She's carrying an umbrella that's as big and black as she is. Marsha sees me, and waves.

"Mercy, T. J., didn't your mother ever teach you to use an umbrella?"

"Hate 'em," I say simply.

She makes a *tisk tisk* sound in the back of her mouth. "Just look at you. Hair standing up all over your head and your shirt slicked down like a seal's coat. Let me get you a towel so you can dry you off."

"I'm fine," I say, a little huffy.

"Yeah? Well, you don't look fine to me. Guess I think it's my job to help 'cause you're here so often."

"No one takes care of me but me. A little water won't hurt."

Through the bars I see her shrug, but her face is all smiles. "You're just another wild animal, that's for sure." She's toying with me again. Marsha always does that.

She fiddles with the lock, the gate creaks open, and I step inside. I scan the park while Marsha pushes herself into the tiny admission booth. The rain's calmed to a light drizzle. All through the zoo, trees bristle from every spot of earth that isn't covered by asphalt. Slick and wet, their leaves have turned the same shiny green as beetle wings. I'm searching for Nancy, but I can't see anyone except the man who sweeps the pathways and the girl who runs concessions. Finally, Marsha slides open the glass window. She's ready for business.

"All right, then. You're the first one in, as usual," she tells me. "You got your pass today?"

My hand's fighting the inside of my damp jeans pocket, which is where I stuck my pass. While I'm tugging on it, I decide to ask Marsha a question. "Do you—do you know a lady named—Nancy Champion?" My mouth feels suddenly tight.

"What did you say?"

"Nancy Champion? She works here. Tall, skinny, brown hair—"

"I know who she is. She a friend of yours? 'Cause I've never seen you talk to anyone in this place."

I'm shaking my head. "No. She's not a friend."

"That's what I thought. So why are you askin' about her?"

I'm not ready for Marsha to act cagey. She's always seemed the kind who would blurt out almost anything.

"It's no big deal," I lie, backing off. "Just forget it."

"Now don't go getting your shorts all tied in a knot," she tells me. "I'm just a naturally curious person. And you askin' about her is one of those psychic things."

And then, the next words out of Marsha's mouth make my stomach lurch into my throat. She jabs a fingernail on the back of my hand and says, "Not fifteen minutes ago, Nancy Champion cornered me in the employees' parking lot and started askin' me all sorts of questions about *you*."

There's a humming in my ears. "About me?"

"Yeah. Nancy says, 'You know that gangly kid, the one on Rollerblades with the dark look on his face?' And I go, 'T. J.? I sure do, he's here every day.' And she says, 'Do you know anything about him?' And I go, 'No, 'cept he's partial to Rafiki and most times stays till closing.' She kept askin' questions, and when I asked her why she wanted to know so bad, she gave me the exact same look that you're giving me now."

I'm starting to shake again, but Marsha keeps chattering, like she doesn't notice a thing.

"Now, what's goin' on?" Marsha asks. "Why is Nancy so fired up about a scowling, animal-nutty, Rollerblading boy like you?"

"Don't know," I shrug.

"Could've told her that you're too stubborn to carry an umbrella in a rainstorm, but I just learned that this morning."

I don't answer. Just stand there, staring. Finally, when my breath feels more even, I say, "I gotta go."

Still, Marsha doesn't notice how this is bothering me. All smiles, she says, "Now, you tell Nancy 'hi' from me when you see her, 'cause she sure is looking for you." She laughs a little, and now I'm inside.

Slip, slip. slip. My skates glide along, shooting pinwheel sprays of water as I keep skating, keep looking. No one's allowed to skate inside the zoo, but the zoo's empty so I'll take my chances. The question is, where do I look? Nancy Champion could be anywhere at all. Make a plan, I tell myself. Start with Rafiki.

The rain must have put Rafiki in a bad mood, because he's really screeching a storm, pumping up and down on his branch like a piston.

"Hey, man, I'm here," I say, extra loud.

Rafiki drops from one arm and swings, the other hand stretched toward me. He wants food. I didn't bring any, which lets me know how rattled I am. I *always* bring him something. He yells again.

"Stop it—you're going to hurt yourself."

It's weird, because suddenly Rafiki settles down. He swings back onto the branch and stares at me.

A strange feeling, like the one I had last night, comes over me. It's like someone's poked a straw in my back, and part of me is getting sucked through it. Nancy. It has to be. I try to act like I don't feel a thing, but after a minute I whirl around.

There's no one there.

A deer's chewing on a tuft of grass, and a knot of zebras huddles against a fence, fit together head to tail as if they were puzzle pieces. No Nancy, no eyes.

I hear myself breathing. Get a grip, I mutter. I start to skate, first to the snake pit, then to the house where they keep the giraffes, on to the seals, the lions, and the elephants. I stop at each place, waiting, watching, wondering where she is and if she's following me. Wondering *why*. Feeling her presence, wanting to yell at the top of my lungs for her to come out, to face me. But, still, she doesn't show.

I'm back to Rafiki, and now my nerves are shot. I sit on a bench. The sun's out; steam rises from the asphalt. My head drops into my hands, and I'm squeezing my temples, pressing so hard that my brain feels like it'll pop. And then I hear it. The same flutey voice I heard yesterday.

"Hello, T. J."

I look up, and there she is, flushed, with a kind of energy that's like she wants to touch me but knows she shouldn't. She's got on the same green uniform, but today every hair is smooth and she smells like apricots.

"Were you looking for me?" She slips down onto the bench beside me.

"No, not really." The second lie of the morning slides out as easily as the first. I feel my heart start to bump.

"Oh? I was looking for you."

My bones feel like ice. No one is around. I'm aware of everything, of the sounds, the air, the smells, the feel of the boards biting my skin, the foot of space between us. I need to understand this woman and what she wants from me.

With my right hand I rub my forearm, trying to gather enough friction to warm up my skin, but it's as useless as striking a soggy match. I'm shaking because I'm wet and cold. At least I think that's why.

"There was a big storm last night. How did you sleep?"

"Okay."

"I couldn't keep my eyes closed. They just kept flying open all night long. So, if you *did* have a bad dream . . . would your mom come in and make you feel better?"

I shouldn't be here. I know it for sure. She's asking me about my mom, and it just feels . . . wrong. No matter if I got to run the whole zoo myself, I was crazy to come.

Now I'm on my feet. "Why do you even care? I don't like questions about my mom, okay? Or me. Or my dad. Leave me alone."

"I'm just trying to get to know you—"

"Why did you ask me to come back? Why did you say I could help you with the animals? What do you want?"

"No. Wait. I'm doing this all wrong. T. J., I know it's going to sound strange, but I want you to trust me enough to answer me this one question."

"Why should I trust you?" My voice sounds hard. "I don't even know you. I don't want to know you."

I'm not prepared for what happens next. Tears roll down her face, but she doesn't even bother to wipe them. They snake down the curve of her cheeks, drop onto her uniform in dark stains, and suddenly I'm thinking of how much she looks like a hurt animal. "What's wrong?" I ask her, speaking as softly as I can.

"I'm sorry, T. J. I know you're confused. One more question, okay? And then I'll tell you my secret. Can you do that little thing for me?"

I feel myself nod.

She swallows, then wipes her face with her fingertips. It's weird, because she seems to be as nervous about this as I am. "T. J.—do you have a birthmark? A strawberry-colored one?"

It's a weird question, but I can't think of any harm it will do if I answer, so I say, "Yeah, on the back of my neck. So what?"

Her skin turns the color of ash. "I need you to do one more thing for me. Turn around and lift up your hair. Let me see it."

"Why?"

"Just do it for me. Please!"

The pink patch of skin's the size of a silver dollar. I twist until my back's to her, then drop my head. My hand pulls damp hair off my skin.

I hear her gasp, "Oh, my Lord."

In an instant I've whirled around. "What?"

"It's you. It *is* you. I knew it, but . . . I can't believe it. After all these years. You're with me again." It's like she's talking to herself and not to me, and now I'm waiting for her to come back from wherever she mentally is, back to the zoo and this bench so she can tell me what the heck is going on.

Finally, I can't take it another minute. "If you don't tell me what this is all about then I'm out of here," I say. I want this to stop, because I'm suddenly scared. She's so intense I can feel the air crack.

Nancy's sliding close to me, and then I feel her hand underneath my chin. She's pulling my face up so she's got me right in her gaze. I'm watching, and it's like her mouth is trying to move, but it can't. I want to jerk free, except I'm locked into her, the same as if she's got chains on me. And then she says, "T. J., before I say anymore, I've got to know, can you keep a secret? Just for a little while? Please, say yes, T. J. It's important."

I don't answer, except to nod.

"I know you don't understand any of this. But . . . T. J. . . . sweetheart, I always hoped this would happen, and now that it has, I can't believe it."

"What?" I demand.

"I gave you up when you were only two days old. But I studied your face before they took you away from me. I knew that somehow I'd see you again. And here you are. Here we are."

The words are starting to swim around me, but she holds me steady. She's pulling me into her now, hugging me so tight I can hardly inhale. I feel her words breathed onto the top of my head, like a blessing. Like a curse.

"T. J."–her fingers grip into my ribs–"T. J., don't you understand? I'm your real mother."

four

"You're a liar," I say. My voice sounds like I'm talking from some-place else. My eyes are buried in her uniform; the green polyester seems to pulse and swirl; I think I'm going to be sick.

"You're my son," she says again, like saying it just makes it so.

I can't take it in. Not the zoo or Nancy or anything that she's saying. I try to pull away, but Nancy's got me locked in her arms and I'm caught as tightly as a fly in a web. One hand is raking through my hair, petting me like I was a baby kitten.

"I'm so happy—I've finally found you! My son, my *son!*" she murmurs, over and over.

"You're *crazy!*" It takes all my strength but I wrench myself free and shoot down the bench, apart from her. Nancy is looking at me, her mouth all wide, like she's going to cry again. She's breathing in and out, puffing the skin on her cheeks, and I think of the side gills on a fish. "T. J., please—I'm your mother!"

"Stop saying that! I don't know you!"

"Yes—but we can change that. Starting now, today! I'm absolutely sure you're mine. I wondered the first day I saw you. Now I'm positive that—"

"You don't know *anything*," I say. Suddenly I hate this woman. Now Nancy's looking lost. Her shoulders droop, and one hand's yanking on the other, like she could pull her fingers right off of her hands. "Sweetheart," she says, "I know this is a shock. It's just—there's no easy way to say it. You're my child."

"My mother is dead!" I blurt out.

"She . . . died?"

"A long time ago."

"I'm so sorry, T. J." Suddenly, her voice drops until it's real low. "Oh, no. T. J., you . . . you knew you were adopted, didn't you?"

I don't answer. I'm trying to think of what to say, trying to make sense of all this. My head hurts. I just want her to disappear, to sink between the painted slats of the park bench and melt into the ground below. I want her to stop saying I'm her son.

"T. J.? Didn't your adoptive mother ever tell you that—"

"Shut up! I wasn't *adopted!*" And then I hiss, "Why are you doing this? What do you want?"

Nancy's quiet for a minute, but her eyes never stop moving over me. I watch her try on different arguments, then cast them aside.

"I'm telling you the truth, T. J. Look at us. We're the same. Our chestnut eyes, our long feet and hands. I've been watching you, the way you move, the way you love animals. You get all of that from *me.*"

That argument is stupid, and I tell her so. "Loving animals doesn't mean anything! Neither do big feet!"

"Then look at this." She flips up her ponytail, and I see a splotch of strawberry color at the base of her neck. "See that? You've got a mark just like it, in the same spot."

I can't help it. My hand flies to the bottom of my neck, right to my birthmark.

"T. J., I remember kissing it, right before they took you away—"

"No!" I scream. I leap to my feet and skate in front of her, trying to hold steady.

"Don't talk to me again," I say. "You're sick." But I feel like I can't get my muscles and bones to work together. I'm like a puppet, and somebody's cut the strings.

"No—wait!" She's reaching out, trying to hold my hand. I won't let her.

"You're hurt and angry. I guess I should have expected that. Just do one thing for me," she pleads. "Don't tell anyone yet. I want to get to know you. I need time. You've got to keep this a secret. Promise me, until we work this out. This is our secret."

"My name is T. J. Lancaster. I'm twelve years old, and my dad's name is Taylor Joseph Lancaster and my mother's name was Cheryl Lancaster. You're wrong. You've mixed me up with someone else. I'm *not* your son. There *is* no secret." I start to skate away, but her voice follows me.

"I'll wait for you, T. J. When you come back, I'll know you're ready."

"I'm not coming back!" I yell to her, to the animals, to the rain that's starting to come down again.

Now I'm skating so fast it's like I'm smoking out of the zoo, breathing hard, moving like a machine. One skate, then the other. Move. Move! The harder I skate, the quicker the thoughts pound through me. I don't know why I'm angry, but I am.

Adopted. My skate smacks the ground. Adopted. Adopted. Everything in my life is changed if that's true. But it's not. She's insane, a liar. My dad would have told me if I'd been adopted. Something like that, something so important, he'd have to say. He couldn't have kept that kind of secret. Not from me. Not from his son.

But would he tell? A voice, one I want to squish so far down I'd never hear it again, starts to whisper to me. Would he tell you, T. J.? He never talks to you. Maybe . . . *No!* I won't let myself think it. Just skate, and leave it behind you. Just skate.

When I get home, I'm panting. My neck feels pinched shut from the lump at the base of my throat. Unlocking the door I skate inside, all the way to my father's den. Midget's loping behind me, trying to say hello, but I just give a quick pat and shove him away. There's something in that den that I need. I throw open the door and skate inside.

From the time I was little, I've always called this small, dimly lit place the Fish Room. All the colors are dark, from the navy plaid curtains to the forest green leather chair. The only light comes from a banker's lamp on my dad's desk and a brass two-bulb fixture on the ceiling. My dad loves to fish, even though he never has the time to, so my mom put up a foot-wide border of rainbow-colored fish along the edge of the ceiling just before she died. Beneath the border hangs a carved wooden sign that says: TIME SPENT FISHING CANNOT BE DEDUCTED FROM A MAN'S LIFE.

For some reason, that sign seems really stupid to me today. Everything gets deducted, 'cause everything counts.

I drop into my father's chair and pull open his drawer, but instead of my dad's personal directory I find a picture that I haven't looked at in a long time. It's of my father and my mother. They're holding on to me, smiling like they just won the lottery. I stare and stare at it, pushing Midget away with my right hand because I want to understand what I'm seeing. Dad, his arm slung around my mother's small shoulders, his blue eyes crinkling at the edges. Mom, her blonde hair curling gently around her face. She's holding on to me.

When I find the number I'm after, I pick up the phone, punching in the numbers before I have a chance to change my mind.

The third ring, and then, "Hello?"

My mouth hardly works.

"Hello?" the voice says again. "Is anyone there?"

"Hi, Aunt Pauline. It's me. T. J." My words sound like all the juice has been squeezed out of them.

"T. J.? Oh, my heavens, T. J.! How are you, darling? It's been years since I've heard from you. Is everything all right?"

"Sure. Sorry I haven't called or written or . . . anything."

Aunt Pauline rushes over me with "Don't worry, we all get busy," and "It's hard to keep in touch, especially with two thousand miles between us," and "How's school? How's your father?" To each question, I give my automatic answers until she's run out of things to ask and I'm tired of stalling. There's a pause, so I make my move.

"The thing I wanted to ask you is, um . . ."

"What is it, T. J.?"

The room seems to push in on me. I know it has to be now, or I'll chicken out and never ask her, so I take a deep breath. "My dad was telling me about my past, about my being . . . *adopted* . . . and all." I say the word "adopted" too loud, so I swallow and try again. "I guess I was wondering if . . . you knew anything about my adoption. Do you, do you know anything about my . . . real mother?"

Aunt Pauline doesn't answer. She doesn't say a thing. How can silence on a telephone mean so much? She must think I'm nuts. Nancy told me a pack of lies, and now my aunt thinks I've been smoking something funny. I'm about to plunge in and tell her it was all a mistake, that I was playing a dumb joke or I had a brain cramp, when it sounds like Aunt Pauline's starting to breathe again. "This is a shock," she says.

"I know—" I begin, but she cuts me off.

"Well, thank the Lord your father finally told you the truth. He swore he never would."

"The . . . truth?" I stammer.

"About your adoption. I'm glad he's come to his senses. I told him it was a mistake to hide something that important from you. Maybe I have a different slant on this because I'm a lawyer, but I think adoptions should *never* be kept secret. Things like this always have a way of coming out."

It's like an electric current is shooting through me, burning a hole right into my stomach. "Do you—do you know who my real mother is?" It surprises me I can even talk. My voice sounds like it's coming from somewhere else.

"I have no idea. But I'm relieved he's opened up to you. The reason he and I don't really talk is because we fought over this very thing. I said, 'Taylor, you've got to be up front with T. J. Adoption is no big deal, but he needs to know.' And he always countered with something like, 'Mind your own business, Pauline. I'll raise my son the way I think best.'"

She's still talking, but right in the middle of her sentence I say thanks and good-bye and hang up the phone. Now it's quiet. I'm sitting in the Fish Room, feeling like I'm floating underwater, and all the world is suddenly out of focus. Midget is whining at my feet.

The picture is staring at me. Instead of smiles, it's like the two of them are laughing at me. We fooled you, they say. Everything you know about you is a lie. You are a lie.

Suddenly, I need to know the color of my mother's eyes. I can't remember. All my memories of her are as flat as the photograph in my hand, and I can't get a grip on it. I rummage through a side drawer until I find what I need. Then I put the picture right underneath the light, holding the magnifying glass directly over my mother's face. Her clear blue eyes stare back at me.

Blue eyes. Hers and my dad's.

How could I have been so stupid not to have known all along? Didn't I learn that genetic stuff just this past year? Two blue-eyed people cannot have a brown-eyed child, right? My mom and my dad could not have had me. The truth had been there all along, but I hadn't seen it.

I throw the picture back into the drawer and slam it shut, hard; Midget jumps like he's been hit.

"So," I say out loud. "So. I'm adopted." And then, like lightning, a truth streaks through me.

My mother had always been a tombstone to me, white marble with carved words over a patch of grass. But now my mother, my *real* mother, is alive. Nancy. I've got a mother. I'm not alone anymore.

I put my head down on my father's desk, and I cry.

five

When I see Nancy, she's got a clipboard dug into her hip and she's scribbling away on some kind of a printed form. It's been three days since I found out the truth. All three days I've been hanging low, trying to figure out what my next move's going to be.

"What's wrong, T. J.?" my dad's been saying the last couple of nights. "You look as white as a sheet."

"I'm just tired," I tell him. "Don't worry about me."

"I had an idea about a job. Instead of a paper route, I was wondering if you'd like to come and do a little work around my office. I'll pay you minimum wage. Son, it's not too soon to think about your future. . . ."

I can't deal with his lectures, so I just tune him out. The thing is, I hate it when he talks to me now. The word "son" sticks in me, like the lie that it is. I want to tell him I know that he's not my father, that he's been lying to me since I was born and that I'll never forgive him for it. But if I told him what I know, it wouldn't be fair, not to Nancy. Because Nancy and me—we've got a secret.

And now, watching Nancy's pen move across the paper, I'm thinking that I've got a chance to belong to someone again. Me and Nancy—we share blood, and that's as tight a bond as any piece of paper saying I belong to my dad.

Still, there are a lot of things that won't line up in my brain.

Even if I get straight on the part of finally having a mother, I look at Nancy and know she's still a stranger to me. How can I skip over twelve years of my life and start today from scratch?

Leaves shimmer in my face like a fountain of green coins, but still I follow every move she makes. I don't know what to do. I want to walk up to her, maybe even put my hand on her arm and touch her, but for some reason I can't. So I just hold back, and watch, like she must have done with me.

She squats down and picks up a piece of dried banana chip that Rafiki's thrown from his cage. I duck further behind the tree, just in case she turns around. The bark bites into my skin and then I hear footsteps. She's walking toward Rafiki's cage.

"Hey, monkeyshines, you've been throwing food again," Nancy calls out. I like the way she talks to Rafiki, same as I do.

Rafiki shrieks like he's laughing.

"Think I got nothing better to do than pick up after you? Not a thing worse than a delinquent monkey. . . ."

Suddenly, she swings around real fast, like she knows something's behind her. This is it, I tell myself—you've got to move. With one hand clinging to the bark of the tree, I step out from behind. Her eyes lock onto mine and she's as still as the wax animals you can buy at the concession stand.

"Hi." I give a little wave. I'm feeling really stupid, same as if all of my clothes disappeared from my body.

Nancy seems to want to run right to me, but I can tell she's holding back. A smile as big as Rafiki's scream breaks across her face. "Well. Hi, yourself," she says.

I take a step. "Don't mind Rafiki. He's—he's always throwing stuff," I say. My feet drag a little with each move I make. "He chucks pieces of orange at every kid that stands too close."

"No kidding. He nailed me with a head of cabbage once."

Her hair's hanging down loose, and she tucks it behind an ear. She looks gangly, awkward, like a bunch of sticks held together with twine.

"Yeah . . . Rafiki, he's got a great arm." The next step is easier, like now my joints are oiled. "The thing is," I tell her, "even if he acts bad sometimes, he doesn't mean it. He—he just doesn't know any better."

"Yeah, I know. He's really very good. I understood it the minute I met him. Rafiki's got to trust people. Maybe someone tried to rush him too fast and he got scared and now he's afraid all the time. But I'm trying to go real slow, so he knows it will be all right. It *will* be all right."

"I know," I say very quietly.

She starts to come toward me. I'm walking the same steady pace that she is. We're close now, and I can't tell what I'm feeling because there're so many things whirling inside of me. Rafiki's quiet, as if he knows not to make a sound. Nancy, eyes bright, holds out a hand to me just like she would to a stray dog. This time she barely touches my hand.

"I'm so glad you came back, T. J."

"Yeah. Me, too," I say. I swallow, and put my hand into hers. Her skin is smooth, but hard, like she's used her hands all of her life. And then, I do something I haven't done since I can remember. I put my arms around Nancy and jump into a hug as if I'd never, ever let go. Now my face is buried into her shoulder and I smell her dusty zoo smell mixed with a faint trace of detergent, and I hear her breathing, her heart beating steady and sure, alive. My throat closes tight, but I swallow past it and look up at Nancy. I'm looking into my own eyes, into a face that's part of me. I'm looking at my mother. I'm finally home.

Have you ever had one of those times when everything seems new? That's how it feels every day that I'm with Nancy.

That first day, when I gave her the hug, I'd noticed it right off. The zoo had suddenly looked different, as if the cage floors had changed to glass and the metal bars had turned to real silver. Every animal had seemed clean and bright and filled with a soul. Even my body felt full, like it'd burst if I took in too deep a breath.

The second day I'd felt it when Nancy—my mom—was humming ahead of me along the path, pulling me into different animal houses and explaining exactly what it is she does for a living. It's like I couldn't take it in fast enough, and the more she showed me the more I wanted to see. I decided that being around her was like taking a long, cool drink of water when you don't even know you're thirsty. At the end of that day I had promised her two things: I'd come back again, and I'd keep our secret forever.

The third day my mom took me to the reptile house. "This is Marlo. She's a boa constrictor with a big appetite." Nancy had stopped and searched my eyes. "Are you okay with reptiles?"

"Sure," I'd said. The truth is, I don't like them much, but decided that if my mom liked them, then I liked them too.

Now it's been a week, and we're back in the reptile house, and my mom's saying, "Here's a gila monster that I look after. I got to name him. I call him Shinto."

A chain of keys dangles from my mom's hip; she unhooks them and opens a cabinet. She grabs a box from a shelf, then unlocks Shinto's glass door and slides it open. Food pellets that look like rabbit droppings make a clicking sound as they drop into his dish.

"You want to try feeding him, T. J.? Shinto's very gentle."

My fingertips lightly touch the spines on Shinto's back. Mom is barely steering my motions, but she's guiding me just the same.

It seems like we're in step together; if I touch something, my mom's right beside me. I notice that our hands are exactly alike. Long fingers with blunt tips, short nails, then small, square palms. Just my mom and me, doing a job. Together.

Now we're at the big-cat house, which is thirty years old so it's made from cement and cinder block and glass. I feel especially bad for Nero, an old, buff-colored male lion with a ratty mane, because he only has a painted cement tree to lie on and a two-foot-deep pond in the corner of his cage. It's so bleak that I wonder why he doesn't go crazy in there. Nero just watches me, twitching his long tail, and I wonder about his pride and if he's ever had cubs and did someone take them away and did he miss them?

My mom's busy with a chart. She's behind me, so I can ask her the next question I've been thinking of, the one I haven't dared say before now.

"Nancy?"

"Humm?"

"Do I . . . do I have a dad?"

I feel her stiffen, but her voice keeps steady. "Of course you have a dad," she says. She puts a little laugh in, but it doesn't sound right. "Everyone has a dad, silly."

Turning, I look right at her. A pink flush has crept up her face.

"Where is he?"

"Gone."

I knew that was what she was going to say, but still, it hurts me. I mean, of course my dad wouldn't stick around, not after dumping me for someone else to raise. It makes sense that he would just walk. He was probably some lowlife, some creep that I'm better off not knowing. What did I expect? I'm blinking, trying to keep myself together, and it makes me mad that I even opened my big mouth. I should've waited. Why did I have to ruin the nice, warm feelings that were just starting to grow inside me?

"He left a long time ago, T. J.," she says quietly.

"Did my dad know about me? I mean, did he know you put me up for—adoption?" She winces, but I have to know that much.

"He knew."

"Oh." I look at my feet. "Well, I figured that. It's no big deal. The thing is, I really don't care."

She seems to get real busy with the chart, jerking it into the cabinet and shutting the door, hard. I stand there, feeling stupid. She moves down to another space, and repeats the procedure. This is the first time she's not looking at me, and I don't like it. I move my mouth to say something, to apologize, but I'm not sure how.

Finally, she decides to talk. "Look, I realize you have a right to know, but this is hard for me. I loved your father very much. He—neither one of us felt we were—ready—to give you the kind of life you deserved. We were both so young."

She looks at me. "Can you possibly understand that?"

I nod, even though I don't.

"I let you go so you'd be happy. Giving you up was the hardest thing I've ever done in my whole life. You were so—innocent. It would have killed me if I'd made the wrong decision."

"You didn't. I'm okay. I'm fine."

"Just tell me, have you been happy, T. J.? Have you?"

"Yeah, I've been great," I lie. I don't want to ruin what we're starting by telling her I've never really been anything but alone. It's still too new. So I smile like I mean it, and she smiles right back, relieved and ready to be cheerful again. I know that we're not going to talk about my father again. Not for a long time.

The rest of the day snaps by. We've been everywhere in the zoo, done everything together. The lady at the concession stand sells us two hot dogs and one large Dr Pepper with two straws and asks, "Who's the kid, Nancy? He looks enough like you to be yours."

"Could be," she says. We grin at each other, and walk on.

When we're by the seal pond, she lets me carry a bucket that's bulging with day-old fish. They smell bad, but Nancy says the seals don't mind. I set it down, then rest my arms on the steel railing, even though the metal's so hot it cooks my skin.

"I want to get to learn all about you," she tells me. "These last few days have been great, but I want more. I want to know what you're thinking. I want to know *you*."

I reach into a bucket and throw a limp fish into a gaping pink mouth. The seal belches, then slaps the water with his fin.

"What can I say?" I answer. "There's not much to tell."

"Of course there is. We've got so much catching up to do. For instance . . . what you like to eat, and what's your favorite subject in school . . ."

"Pizza and math. But it's got to be pepperoni or forget it."

"Really? Me, too. I *love* pepperoni," she says, and gives a squeal. For a second she sounds like a little girl instead of a mother, and I wonder how old she really is.

"I'll eat the stuff for breakfast," she goes on. Jabbing a finger in the air, she declares, "For us, it's pepperoni or nothing!"

"It's all we'll eat!" I beam. Another link. One cord, then another, looped and tied, pulling us together. It's more than just having things in common, like animals and pizza. We share blood. We're connected.

It's five o'clock, and the day's winding down. We're back at the lion house and she turns to me, her face suddenly serious. Her look scares me. The first thought in my head is, what have I done wrong? For some reason I'm really afraid that she's not going to want to see me again.

"You realize we've been together all week?"

I nod. I know that more than I've ever known anything.

"Thanks so much for spending all this time with me," she tells me. "It's been perfect."

That sounds final. My heart's sinking. Maybe that's all it's going to be. Maybe she'll tell me to go home now, like a lost cat, fed and cleaned, then delivered right back to its owners.

"Can you come back tomorrow?"

"Sure," I say, relieved.

Her uniform has a stain, right by her belt, where she lost some mustard off her hot dog. I'm about to say something smart about it when she says, "T. J., I need to ask you a favor."

"Yeah? What kind of favor?" I sound cagey, but the truth is, I'd already give her anything.

"I want you to come with me to a special place. I have one more secret that I want to show you tomorrow. That's my day off." She's looking at me, squinting because the sun's in her eyes. "What do you say?"

My heart freezes. Another secret? I don't want another one, because I'm barely getting used to this one.

Her finger lightly touches the tip of my nose. "Don't look so scared," she says. "I promise—it's a good secret."

"Then . . . why don't you tell me now?"

"Lots of reasons. For one thing, I've got to get going. I've got a life outside this place. For another, I think we're off to a great start. I don't want to say any more just yet."

"But—"

"Just come back tomorrow," she says, smoothing my hair. "One more big secret, and you'll know everything. So, you'll be here?"

"Yeah. Sure," I say. I'm watching her break into a smile, but for once, I don't shadow her. Another secret. Another night before I find out if my new life is going to change again.

SIX

I'm surprised how nervous I feel, riding alone with my mother in her beat-up blue Jeep. Every bump she hits on the road makes my teeth jar, but after awhile she just reaches over and pats my hand, like that'll smooth everything.

"Sorry, for the rough ride, honey," she says. "This old thing needs new shocks. What kind of car does your dad drive?"

It makes me embarrassed, but I have to answer. "A BMW. It's old, though." I don't tell her we've only had it two years, and that my dad's ready to trade it in for a new one.

"Wow," she says. "A beemer. Holy cow."

"Yeah. Well," I say. And then my voice just kind of dies out.

Glare from the sun makes it hard to see where we're going, and my mom isn't saying. She starts humming a song I don't know, and I settle in, content. It's strange, the way we don't have to talk to each other. We've only been together eight days and already it's starting to feel the littlest bit like we're a family. It's a kind of warm feeling that spreads to the edges.

I kick an empty Mountain Springs water bottle to the side and try to find a place to stretch my feet. There's all kinds of dented cans, newspaper stacks tied with string, and bags filled with empty milk jugs all over the place.

I'm still trying to find a spot, so I'm making a lot of crunching noises. My mom looks over.

"Sorry—I'm taking those to a recycling place. I recycle everything I can," she says. "Our planet can't take being polluted much longer before it just chokes on itself. Do you recycle, T. J.?"

"Sure," I nod. I don't really, but I'm going to start.

"Good. I knew you would. You just seem like that type of kid to me."

She's smiling like I just told her I was going to Harvard instead of throwing a bunch of cans into a bin. What a strange woman my mother has turned out to be. Who knows what she'll think is a great surprise? Now I really want to know what she's going to spring on me, just so I can be prepared.

"Why can't you tell me what this is all about?" I ask.

"Because then it wouldn't be a surprise, now would it? You'll just have to trust me."

We're getting farther and farther away from the zoo, and I'm getting anxious. The houses in these neighborhoods are ratty and small, with bunches of dirty-looking kids hunched on the grass like clumps of weeds. I think my mom can sense the way I'm feeling, 'cause suddenly she changes her mind.

"Okay, T. J., I guess I can tell you part of the surprise. I'm taking you to where I live. I have to warn you that it's not much, especially next to what you're probably used to. But it's home." She looks over at me, her face suddenly serious. "There's one thing you should know about me, T. J. I've always paid my own way."

"That's cool," I tell her. "Besides, I don't care what your house looks like. I'm not a snob."

Her hand flutters against my arm. "I'm thinking that if you know where I live, maybe you can come see me."

"So, the surprise is your house?"

"It's part of the surprise, but not the biggest part. You'll have to wait for the rest."

I'm groaning, 'cause I've never been too good at waiting for things. My mom breaks in and says, "Quit your bellyaching. Look—we're here."

The car shudders to a stop. I squint as I peer out the window, and then I realize that I'm looking at a dump. Even though I told her I wasn't a snob, I still can't believe my mother lives in a place like this. The grass out front is crisped all along the west side, with dandelions and burn holes as big as pie tins through what's left of the front. Beyond the lawn is the smallest house I've ever seen. Wood that used to be white but now's faded to gray; a saggy couch resting on a cement porch; a wrought-iron railing bleeding rust down concrete steps.

My mom's waiting for me to say something, so I make my mouth turn up in a smile and I look right at her. I can tell that it's real important to her that I like this place.

"What do you think, T. J.? Is it too slummy for you?"

"Nope," I say. "It's great. I like the . . . porch." Even from the Jeep I can see a couple of paperback books stacked on the sofa cushions, so I say, "I bet you like to sit out there and read. I read a lot too."

"Yeah, well, reading takes me away." She leans back into her seat and blows a puff of air between her lips. "This place needs a lot of work. I'm going to get to this yard one of these days, but it's just—life. You know?" Then, as quickly as it darkened, her face clears. "But, like I said, this isn't the surprise." My mom smacks her palms against the steering wheel and looks at me. "Now wait here until I call you inside. Don't move, okay? When I call your name, you just walk right on in."

"Okay," I tell her. "I can do that."

She's almost skipping as she runs up the two steps and pulls open the front door. After she's been gone a few minutes, a puffy-looking lady walks out of my mother's house, muttering something that from where I am sounds an awful lot like a curse. The old lady stares at me; her eyes narrow into slits, which tells me she thinks I'm the type of kid who would spray graffiti on her house. I'm really hoping she's not the surprise, because I don't like her already. A week ago, I might have given the finger to anyone who looked at me that way, but now I have to think things through. The lady's still staring, so I just give her a quick nod and look away. She gives what sounds like a cough, and I watch her clomp to the house next door and slam the screen behind her. What an old bat.

Now I'm standing on the sidewalk, twisting my fingers together, knocking a rock with the toe of my shoe. Waiting, with my eyes glued to my mother's front door. Finally I hear, "T. J.–it's time! Come on in!"

I don't know what I'm expecting as I go up those stairs and pull open the door. It's dim inside, with lots of plants hanging in front of windows or drooping off. I hear my mom calling me to come into the kitchen, which, she says, is right ahead of me and to keep walking straight.

I see my mom, and then I see something else. A girl, maybe eight years old, standing right in front of my mother. My mom's got her hands on either side of the kid's neck, as if the girl's head'd fall off unless my mom holds it there. My mom's all tense, but she's smiling big.

"Londyn," she says, "Londyn, this is T. J."

"Hi," the kid says in a raspy voice. She's got dark hair that hangs loose to her elbows, a white T-shirt, and a pair of faded-out jeans. She smiles a goofy smile. Her front teeth are too big for her face.

"Hi yourself," I answer. Then I look at my mom's eyes, and

she's all misted up like she's going to cry. "T. J., Londyn is your surprise. She's—she's your little sister. You've got your very own sister. Isn't that great?"

I don't make a sound.

My mom's rubbing at the skin underneath her eyes. "All my life, I've dreamed that you two would meet, and now it's happened. We're together. We're a family."

A sister. Great. I guess my first thought is that I've been robbed. It's not a nice thing to think, but that's what's going through my mind. I've had my mom for exactly eight days, have just barely gotten to know a few things about her, and now I have this extra person to deal with. Like I said, I don't much like kids, and this one looks kind of dumb. Her mouth hangs open and when she breathes she sounds like there's a whistle caught in her throat. Suddenly, Londyn runs over and gives me a hug. She's squeezing so hard the air practically pops out of my chest.

"I'm glad you're here. I'm glad I've got a brother," she says into my shirt.

I'm not sure what I'm supposed to do. My mom's watching me, her eyes locked onto mine. Be nice, they seem to beg. Squeeze her, hug her. Have a Kodak moment.

But I can't. I stand like a statue, except Londyn won't give it up. Finally, 'cause I don't know what else to do, I pat the top of the kid's head, same as I would Midget. This seems to make Londyn happy because she looks up, right into my eyes, and then she raises on tiptoe and kisses the tip of my chin.

That's when I lose it. Nobody kisses me. Even though I don't mean to, I jerk the same way I do when a doctor smacks my knee with one of those rubber hammers. My mom looks hurt, but Londyn, who by now I think really *is* dumb, just giggles into her hands.

"I'm glad I've got a brother," Londyn says again. "A brother. A brother! I got me a brother!"

I don't know why, but it's really starting to annoy me, the way she says the same thing over and over again.

"A brother, a brother—"

"Yeah, and I got me a sister," I snap. "I get the point, Londyn."

Everything stops now; the two of them just stare, blinking. I'm trying to decide what I'm supposed to do next, but I'm too off balance to think straight. Finally, my mom says, "Londyn, sweetie, could you go to Mrs. Nichols's house for a little while? I want to talk to T. J. for a minute."

"But she just left here. I don't want to see Mrs. Nichols again. She's crabby."

"Londyn—please!"

"Okay," she wheezes. Then she coughs so hard it sounds like her lungs are full of jelly. "But can I see T. J. when I get back?"

"I guess that's up to T. J."

It's my move, so I clear my throat. "Sure, I'll wait," I say, trying to look like I almost halfway mean it. I try to smile.

"Then I'll see 'ya real soon, brother," she chirps. "Don't go away, okay?"

"I won't." I give half a wave. "Bye."

The screen door slams shut, and then it's quiet. Too quiet. My mom's face is going hard, and I know she thinks I should have been nicer to the kid. I feel like this whole thing was some kind of test that I failed. Does that mean she's not going to like me anymore? That's the part that makes me nervous.

"Well, that didn't go so great. Sit." My mom motions me into a vinyl chair. The table is the old kind, with silver legs and a scratched-up top that is supposed to look like wood but is really plastic.

She drops into a chair beside me, chin in hand, sagging the middle of her white T-shirt. "I'm sorry. I guess I should have told you first."

I shrug my shoulders. Somewhere in the kitchen a clock is ticking. It's a big plastic wall clock shaped like a cat. I hate it.

"It's just . . . I didn't know. I mean, you told me in your other house there was just you and your dad, and I . . ." she falters. "I thought, maybe, you'd be happy."

Snorting, I say, "Why would another kid make me happy?"

"Why? *Why?*" Her fingertips dig into her cheek. "Because Londyn is your sister. You're not an only child anymore. Think of it, T. J. You have a family. A sister is a special gift."

I sit there, speechless. So, I have a sister. What am I supposed to say about it? It kind of makes me mad, the way my mom's expecting me to act like we're on some talk show and I'm supposed to cry now. I don't want to do anything except maybe punch a wall, so I fold into myself, waiting for the anger to pass. For the first time in a week, I wish I didn't have to be with my mother.

Nancy seems to be reading my mind, because now her hand is on top of mine. "T. J., are you okay?"

"I guess."

"Look, Londyn is a great kid. Can't you just give her a chance?"

Nodding, I push the cuticles back on my fingers. There's a little half moon of dirt under my thumbnail. I pick at it. The cat clock ticks the seconds away, but my mom's staying as quiet as I am, shifting, settling in. My dad—my adoptive dad—can't stand it when I'm quiet. He has to fill the space, pecking at my stillness with a bunch of words. But my mom just breathes softly, waiting. She's not going to talk, so finally I do.

"So. Who's the dad?" I ask, still playing with my nail. "Is

he around? Or did Londyn's dad leave her, too?"

"He left."

I don't know why, but that makes me feel better.

Squinting at the corner of the room, my mom looks lost in thought. "His name was Phil. Philip Champion. I met him when I was a student in England. He's from London. That's where I got your sister's name. Only I changed the *O* to a *Y*. Her name's spelled L-o-n-d-*y*-n."

"Does this Phil guy ever come to see her?"

My mom shakes her head. "He took off right after she was born. I haven't seen him since. He just . . . disappeared."

"That happens to you a lot, doesn't it? You've been with two guys that dumped you? Geeze, Nancy, you must not be a very good judge of men." As soon as the words are out of my mouth I wish I could take them back, suck them up, and swallow them in. How much of my smart mouth will my mom be willing to take? But instead of smacking me one, she grips my hand even tighter.

"T. J.," she says. "T. J.—it's only happened to me once. Your father is Philip Champion, too."

"What?" It's hard for me to squeeze that small word out. "What?"

"That's why I want you to understand how much this means to me. You and Londyn are full brother and sister. That's the secret. You two belong together."

My knees suddenly feel wobbly even though I'm sitting down. In a flash I can see it: Londyn's dark hair, same as mine, and the perfect mirror of my eyes, except hers are open where mine are guarded. She really is my sister! There is someone else who is just like me, sharing more blood between us than any other two people on the planet.

And then, just as fast, a thought hits me like an open-handed slap. We both had the same dad, and I came first. My mom kept Londyn, but she gave me away.

And I want to know why.

seven

"T. J., where have you been? Don't tell me you were at that zoo again."

It's my dad. He's pacing around the living room in tight circles, like a caged Bengal tiger. He's got a cola in his hand, and the ice cubes click against the glass as he speaks. "Do you have any idea what time it is?"

"Sorry," I murmur. Dropping my skates onto the tile floor, I turn to walk up the stairs. I don't want to talk to him now. I don't want to talk to anyone. I just want to sit in a quiet spot and think over what's happened to me.

His voice floats over my head. "T. J., wait. Where are you going?"

"To my room."

"You may be done talking to me, but I'm not done with you. Look at me. I am your father!"

I turn. My dad's face is balled up, the first sign that he's getting mad. The only thing that goes through my mind is that this man isn't really my dad. He picked me up at the hospital the same way a customer buys a pet from the store, and then lied and called me his son.

Stabbing a finger at his own watch, he barks, "You didn't put your watch on, did you?" He looks at my bare wrist. "I thought so. It doesn't matter what I say, does it? We talk about you being late, you tell me you'll do better, and before you know it we're back to the same—"

"Look, I don't feel good," I break in. "I'm going to go lie down."

Even though my dad is old, he can move fast. In a flash he's right beside me. "Just a minute. You do look—strange. What's wrong?" He touches my cheek with the back of his hand; his skin feels cool, so I must be flushed. Searching my eyes, he asks, "Is it your stomach?"

"No. My head." That much is true. Thoughts have pounded through my skull, and it aches, all the way down my neck.

"How bad? Should I call the doctor—"

"No. I'm fine. Just let me go to bed."

It's an effort to speak, and sensing it, my dad lets me leave. Midget trots after me as I shut my door and flop across my bed. My drapes have stayed shut all day, so it's dark in here, same as I'm feeling. Spike, my parrot, squawks at me because he doesn't like to be left in the dark. I tell him to shut up.

Midget jumps on the bed and starts nibbling the nape of my neck, and it's giving me chill bumps. It's Midget's way of comforting me; his white teeth click against me in tiny little bites. Most of the time I let him, but not tonight.

"Go away, Midget," I say, pushing at him. I'm not in the mood to play with my dog. I have to think. But Midget's ninety-pound bulk cannot be budged, no matter how hard I push, so he just grunts and drops beside me and then I feel him settle in, pressing his ribs into mine. Rolling over, I stare at my cream-colored ceiling.

I don't want to think about it, but I can't get the words and pictures of this morning out of my head. When I squeeze my eyes shut I'm right back in that tired-looking kitchen, watching my mom's mouth move as she goes on and on with her story.

She'd tried to find the right words, but there'd been no good way to say it. She hadn't been married, so after I was born Phil had convinced her to give me up, sign me over, send me away so someone else could take care of his mistake. What a jerk he must have been.

"How could you let him make you do it?" I'd demanded.

"I don't know . . . how can I explain something like that? He wasn't ready. I wasn't ready. He—I loved him."

"You loved *him*. But you didn't love *me?*"

My mom had looked like I'd stabbed her with a hot knife. "You'll never know how much you meant to me. You were *part* of me! I even named you. To me you were James. I held you and . . . I kissed you. Giving you up was the hardest—the worst—thing I've ever done!"

Then my mom had told me how she and Phil stayed together after they'd unloaded me. They'd actually gotten married, and everything went fine until she got pregnant with a new kid. This time Phil hopped a plane back to England, leaving my mom to take care of a new baby girl. Londyn. She kept Londyn.

That's the part I just can't get over, that sticks in my throat like a bone. *I'm* signed away after a couple days, but my mom decided *Londyn* was her one chance at a family. Real nice. The firstborn was tossed out, but the second child was saved.

After my mom had finished telling me about her past, after she'd wiped underneath her eyes with a crumpled napkin, I'd just stood up and asked to leave.

"Wait. T. J.," my mom had cried, "can't you try to understand? I was *young*. I did what I thought was best. Let's just forget the past and pick up from here."

"I need to get back," I'd told her. "My dad gets worried if I'm gone too long." I was hoping that comment would sting.

"But Londyn will be so disappointed." She'd looked at me like she was deciding if she should say something.

"What? Is there more?" If she'd known me better, she would have been able to tell that I was barely keeping it in. I mean, I understood all along that she'd given me up. But to dump me and keep my sister . . .

"Well, I—I thought, no . . . ," she'd said, shaking her head. "Never mind. This probably isn't the right time."

But by then I was figuring I'd had it up to here with secrets, and if there were more she'd just better spit them out, so I'd said, "Look, you might as well finish this. I *want* you to tell me."

She'd given me a half smile and said, "It's just that you and Londyn belong together, and I was thinking that maybe you could . . . baby-sit Londyn for the summer here in my house. I mean, if you wanted. I thought that way, you could learn more about your sister, and about me. Our next-door neighbor's been watching her, but Londyn hates Mrs. Nichols—"

In that instant, it had all come clear. I saw what she'd been after. No wonder she'd been following me, sucking me into her life. She wanted me as a stinking baby-sitter for the kid she kept.

"Is that why you brought me here?" I'd yelled, practically spitting out the words. I'd felt my pulse pound in my neck. "So I could *baby-sit?* You think since I'm related, maybe I won't charge or something?"

"No. NO!" She'd shaken her head really fast. "You don't understand what I'm trying to say! T. J., I wouldn't—I didn't—"

That's when I'd decided to just blow her off and leave, before I said something really bad. I had to get control, to pull it all back inside, so I'd walked out and sat in my mom's Jeep and had taken so many deep breaths I'd thought I might pass out. In a few minutes she'd come out and driven me back to the zoo. The whole drive had been in silence except for the sniffs from my mom. From the corner of my eye I watched her rub her nose with a Kleenex, like she was sad that the tears came out of her and not me. I guess I looked angry enough to scare her, so she'd left me alone, which was what I wanted.

I'd been hopping out of her car when she'd reached over and grabbed me by the arm. "Don't shut me out, T. J.," she'd pleaded. The skin around her nose had been rubbed raw. "It's taken me this long to find you. I can't stand to lose you again."

"You didn't lose me, Nancy," I'd said, shaking off her arm. "You gave me away."

After that I'd grabbed my Rollerblades that I'd stashed with Marsha, and I'd skated around, feeling the bumps under the wheels and the hot summer wind drying my skin, until I'd finally realized I had nowhere else to go but home. If this *is* home. I don't know where I belong anymore.

Now I flip onto my stomach and stare at my wooden headboard. When I was a kid, I carved my initials on the side post, and then put the date underneath. The letters look like toothpicks. I touch them with the tips of my fingers.

Time. I wish I could go back to when I'd carved those letters. I didn't know anything then. I didn't know that people could have you and just give you up. When I was small I believed that everything would turn out okay. I even prayed to God. Now I don't know how I feel about God, except that if He *is* there, He's sure made a mess out of my life. But I can't help thinking about what it was like back then, and I don't know what else to do, so I send up a halfhearted prayer. I'm not saying it out loud, but in a whisper, so soft I can barely hear it myself.

"God, whoever you are, if you really do listen or care . . . give me a sign. I—I don't know what to do."

It's real quiet. I don't know what I'm waiting for, exactly. I don't think it'll be lightning, but I'm half expecting something. Then Midget burps. Great. Some sign. That's what you get for praying.

Suddenly I hear a knock on my door—three short thumps, the way my dad always does. When the door creaks open, a knife of light falls across me.

"T. J., before you go to sleep, I have to tell you that there were two calls left for you on the answering machine. Some woman named Nancy."

"Oh," I say. Having him say her name makes my stomach twist.

"She wants you to phone her back. Lord, it's dark in here," he says. He flips on the light, and I squint. Spike squawks and puffs his feathers, clawing his perch to show he's annoyed at the illumination.

My dad walks over to hand me a number that he's scrawled on a pink slip. "Nancy called at three fifteen." "Nancy called at five o'clock. Wants you to return calls."

I take the piece of paper, the kind that secretaries use in a business office. Leave it to my dad to have a special pad for messages.

"Thanks," I say. I look at the paper, at my mother's name written in square, black-ink letters. I don't know how I feel about Nancy calling me here, except that it seems strange.

"So, who is this woman?" my dad asks. He sits down on the end of my bed. I feel the mattress strain under his weight, feel myself shift toward him.

"Nobody. Just a lady I met at the zoo."

"Why did you give a strange woman your phone number? In this day and age, that can be dangerous."

"She's not crazy. She works there."

"What does she want from you?"

"Nothing."

"Are you in some sort of trouble?"

My dad's got his arms crossed over his chest, right where his paunch begins to swell. He's looking at me as if he's decided that I've done something wrong. Like he wants an explanation. I don't want him guessing anything, so I just say, "Okay. Her name is Nancy. She wants me to baby-sit her kid, that's all. She thought I was the responsible type. I'm not going to do it."

"This Nancy person wants *you* to baby-sit?"

"Yeah."

"How many kids?"

"One. An eight-year-old girl."

"Is this for money?"

"Of course it's for money," I snap.

"How much?"

"I didn't ask. I don't want to do it, so it doesn't matter."

"Hmm," my dad says, rubbing his chin. "Interesting. You'd only have to watch one little kid, and you'd get paid." He leans forward, so that his elbows drill his knees. "Which would you rather do—work in my office with me, or baby-sit?" When he straightens, the white stubble of his beard catches the overhead light. "I told you, I want you to get a job. Now's the time to do it. If you'd come to work at my office—"

"No. I don't want to spend my days inside."

For a second, he looks disappointed. Then his face clears. "Take the baby-sitting job."

My mouth drops open, just a little. I can't believe my dad would even consider letting me baby-sit. I mean, he's always giving me grief about my earring. He said it made his son look like a girl. Well, watching a kid sure as heck seems like a girl thing to me. But for some reason, my dad's looking pleased with the idea.

"Look," I tell him. "This is *my* summer. I don't have time to sit and watch an eight-year-old brat. No, thanks."

"Oh, you don't?" He fiddles with the zipper on his jogging suit. "Well," he says, "you've got time to stare at a bunch of monkeys for free. I'd say you have time for a real job."

"But I don't need the money," I say to the ceiling. "And I don't like kids."

"You've got money because I gave you that allowance. Maybe that's been a mistake. I thought handling it would teach you responsibility, but maybe you need some *real* life experience. A job might bring you out of that shell of yours."

I snort my answer, but my dad keeps talking.

"At least you'd be paid for your time. Even though you only spend a hundred dollars here and another hundred there, it all adds up. You only need to spend a hundred dollars ten times—"

". . . and you've gone through a thousand dollars," I finish for him. Shows how many times I've heard that. But I have three thousand dollars collecting interest in my savings account. My dad's given me fifty bucks a week since I can remember, and there's not much I want, so it keeps adding up. Like I said, money is not a problem for me.

I close my eyes. Maybe if I look sleepy, he'll go away, and I can think again. But his voice drills into my mind.

"T. J., I'm talking about you connecting to the world we live in."

"Right."

"You're so moody. You're twelve years old, and you act like you've already seen it all. Maybe hard work would turn you around." He slaps his hands on his thighs. That means he's made up his mind. "You have two choices. You can come to work with me, or you can take the baby-sitting job."

He waits for me to say something, but I'm as still as the walls. Like I said, I'm not sure how I feel about God, but now, lying here on my bed, a thought jumps at me. Maybe this is the sign. I mean, a minute ago I was trying to decide if I even want to see my mom again, and all of a sudden I'm being pushed right into her world. Toward my mom, toward my sister. And away from my dad.

It's weird. I think of pushing back against what my dad wants and my mom and my sister want from me. But instead of fighting, I decide to let it go. To ride the current, to relax and let myself float along. Maybe all this was meant to be. Maybe I'm *supposed* to watch Londyn.

"So, what do you say? Me, or the eight-year-old?"

"I'll call Nancy," I tell him. "I can always quit if I don't like it."

"Way to go, son. You're growing up." He's beaming at me, and I feel a pang of guilt. He's got no idea of what he's just told me to do.

"How's that headache?"

"Gone," I tell him. I'm surprised, because now that I've decided to watch Londyn, my headache really has disappeared.

It's got to be a sign.

eight

I'm standing at our living room window, ready to bolt out the door the second I catch sight of my mom's car. The timing of this has got to be just right; if my dad leaves early like he does most every morning, then they should just miss each other. But I hear my dad in the kitchen, dinking around with his onion bagel, and the clock's ticking closer to eight.

Right now, the most important thing is that my mom and my dad don't see each other. I'm not ready for them to meet, not yet, and maybe not ever. I wonder if my father could look at my mom and guess. Would he see in her the same dark eyes and lean frame that I have? Would that tell him we are mother and son? The thought scares me, because I know one thing as sure as I know anything: If my dad figures out who Nancy is, he'll break things up between us hard and fast.

I'm remembering how once, two years ago last Christmas, our housekeeper helped herself to an extra twenty-five dollars from the petty cash jar my dad keeps in the kitchen. When my dad found out, he'd stuck the jar right under her nose and demanded the money back.

"It's just a couple of bucks to tide me over until the season's done," she'd said. "Christmas breaks me every year."

"It's not the fact that you need the money, Clara," my dad had stormed. "You could have come to me, and I would have given it to you. It's the fact that you *took* the money. I will not tolerate a thief. Get your belongings and leave."

The thing I remember most is that he made Clara take every last trace of herself, down to the cookies she'd baked that day. It's like he wanted to rub out any reminder that she'd ever even been in our home.

Now, as I remember Clara crying and the way she had to pack up those still-warm cookies, I'm thinking about what a big chance I'm taking here. I've absolutely got to keep my mom and Dad apart. A patch of blue's moving up our street, the color of my mom's Jeep, but it moves on, not turning in. Branches arch across the bay window, and the leaves are tipped with drops of dew that blink in the morning sun. I'd think the whole thing was pretty if I didn't have to see through those leaves. Right now, if I had a chain saw I would cut down the whole stinking wall of trees. The same trees that keep the neighbors from looking into the Lancaster home keep the Lancasters from seeing out.

"First day on the job, and you're rarin' to go," my dad says from behind me. I whip around and there he is, all shined up for a day at the office. His skin has a polish to it in the morning, and every hair has been put in its place. His clothes are perfect: starched white shirt under a three-piece suit pressed into knife pleats. It looks as though he's busted out of a shrink-wrapped package.

"Oh, hi," I say.

"So. Do I get to meet this woman?"

My heart thumps when he says that. He must have seen me tense, because he says, "T. J., what's going on here? You're as jumpy as a cat. Is there something you're not telling me?"

"No. Everything's fine," I say into the glass. My breath makes a foggy circle, so I stand back, just a bit. "You can't meet her because Nancy's coming at eight, and you have to go to work before that."

"Oh, I don't know. I own the company," says my dad, and all the while I'm hugging myself so tight I can feel my ribs underneath my fingers.

And then he says exactly the words I did not want him to say. "Maybe I'll stay here and meet this Nancy person."

Now I'm yelling right into the window. "Why? So you can check up on me? You always have to get into my life, Dad. This is just a baby-sitting job, no big deal, so leave it alone."

I look back just in time to watch my dad's smile fade. I can tell he's trying to be nice, to be supportive of his kid's first job. What he doesn't understand is that I've got a secret, and I have to do what it takes to keep it that way.

"Sorry, Dad," I say, and I really am. "Look, you go on. I'll have you meet Nancy another time."

"Can I at least have her last name?" From his breast pocket, he produces a small day-timer. He clicks his pen and looks at me, poised, ready to write.

Even though I know I'm pushing it, I ask, "What for?"

"In case I need to get in touch with you." My dad's tone is guarded, and I realize I've really blown it with him. For a second I start to feel bad, and then I shake it off. It doesn't matter. I have my mom now, and I can take it if he gets a little bent out of joint.

"Her name is Nancy Champion," I say. I take a breath, and wait to see if the name means anything to him, but he just scrawls the letters down. After I give him the number, he tucks the book back inside his pocket and then picks up his briefcase to leave.

"Good luck, son."

"Thanks," I say.

Then he's gone. Nine minutes after he's left, Nancy pulls up. Once I'm in her car, I've left the other life behind. I'm with my mom again. We're on our way home.

. . .

I haven't been in my mom's Jeep more than one minute when I figure she's having second thoughts about me being in charge of Londyn. It's in the way she's fidgeting. Her left hand's drumming the steering wheel, while her right's clutching it with a white-knuckle grip.

"Londyn's excited about this," she tells me. "So am I. We're so happy you changed your mind."

I shrug and look out the window. But my mom won't let it go. "You're okay with everything? It's just that the last time we were together, you were so upset—"

"It's over," I snap. "You did what you did. I just want to get on with it. Is that okay with you?"

"Fine."

"Fine," I repeat.

"I'm glad you're giving us another chance." A breath, and then, "Now, you're sure you can handle this?"

"I'm sure."

A pause, and then, "T. J., if it gets bad, you can always bring her to the zoo. Call me. I'll come pick you up—"

"Look, I can handle Londyn." Truth is, I want to try this on my own. I want my mom to think I can do things really well. I want her to be proud of me, to trust me.

My mom shrugs the tiniest little shrug, which seems to be for her and not for me. Taking a sip of coffee out of a gray thermos cup, she says, "All right. If you're sure. Oh, did I tell you that Londyn's got asthma? I can't remember if I did or not."

"No," I answer. That piece of information makes me uneasy. Watching a little kid's one thing. Watching a sick little kid is something else again. "How bad?" I ask.

"Just a touch. Dust bothers her some, so I try to keep things clean, but it's hard, you know? With work and a kid and a house and paying the bills, well, it gets away from me sometimes."

"Does she have a special doctor I should call in case something happens?" Right then I'd wished I'd had a notebook to write the number on, just like my dad.

"Nope. No special doctor." My mom straightens her back. "Look, T. J., I can't afford a lot of medical bills, so Londyn and I, we just sort of . . . manage. I barely make enough to scrape by, and there's not much left at the end of the month. It's the best I can do. Make sure her inhaler is close by and everything will be fine, okay?"

We bounced along for at least a mile before she speaks again. "By the way, that's some house you live in."

"It's okay."

"Okay. *Okay?* It's as big as the entire zoo. You've got money."

"Some."

"I'm glad you were placed in a good home," she says softly. "Really, really glad."

We drive for a while and I start to remember the area. From the sorry state of the homes around me, I'd say we're close to my mom's street. We reach a corner that says Blossom Avenue. My mom slows and turns on it, but there're no flowers around here at all. Maybe whoever named it thought if they slapped the word "blossom" on the street, the blooms would just naturally follow. They didn't.

My mom's pursing her lips, which means to me she's still worrying about something.

"Can I ask you a question?"

"Yeah. Sure."

"Have you ever had to work before? I mean, to get something you really wanted?"

I bristle inside. "I know how to work, if that's what you're asking."

"But you've never *had* to, right?"

The way she said it wasn't exactly a question, so I just play with the seat-belt buckle so that my eyes won't be on her face.

"You've got to understand that it's not that way for me. When my money's gone, it's gone. I live a different life than you're used to. I—I hope you can deal with that."

She's pulled into her driveway and slips the gearshift into park. I can tell from her expression she's looking at her house through my eyes, and she's noticing how ratty it looks. I don't want her to think about it, so to change the subject I say, "Where's the kid?"

"I left Londyn asleep in bed. Don't worry, she's used to being alone for a few minutes. I've locked the door, so here's the key." She reaches over and presses it into my hand. "Call if you need anything at all."

"Okay."

I'm about to get out when she leans over and gives me the tiniest little kiss, right on my cheek, as light as dandelion fluff.

"Thanks, T. J.," she says, her face close to mine. "Thanks for giving me another chance at this."

"No problem," I say. I wish I could come up with something better than that to tell her, but at times words come hard to me, and this is one of those times.

"And thanks for watching Londyn. She needs you. She needs a big brother."

Clearing my throat, I try to lighten the mood. "I'm getting used to the idea of a kid sister," I tell her. "Always wanted someone I could boss around."

My mom's nose crinkles with her smile. I hop out, and with a flutter of her long fingers, she's gone.

. . .

"My brother T. J. is here!" Londyn caws. She's awake, waiting for me in an oversized T-shirt, and the legs beneath the thin, sagging hem are even thinner than mine were when I was her age. Her hair is sticking up in dark clumps, like a ball of black yarn, but she's got no sense at all about how rumpled she looks. She's just runs right into me and tries to take a hug.

I give her a halfhearted squeeze, but I know this lovey stuff is something I'll have to nip in the bud. I push her back, which isn't hard because she probably weighs only fifty pounds, and I say, "Listen, Londyn, there's one thing you've got to get straight about me. I don't want to hurt your feelings, but—I'm not the huggy type."

Londyn just giggles. "I'm hungry," she says.

"I know. But about what I just said about not being the huggy type? That means I want you to give me my own space."

She looks at me, blank as a piece of white paper.

I try again. "Don't go jumping all over me, okay?"

"Okay."

And then, as if she didn't hear a word I just said, she takes my hand and leads me into the kitchen. I decide to let her, just this once. Don't want to start off the morning by arguing with her, and I'll teach her what kind of rules we're going to live by in stages. Londyn gives a little half skip as she leads me to the cupboard and points to where the cereal is.

"I'd like some Cheerios, please," she says.

In a hearty voice, I answer, "One bowl of Cheerios, coming up."

She seems to be happy, and that means my job is going to be an easy one. All I have to do now is feed her. How hard can that be?

Fifteen minutes later I still can't get the little twerp to eat her cereal. If I were in my dad's home, I would have just dumped the whole bowl down the drain and started over. But I can't help thinking about what my mom said about money, and I can't help worrying that if I let this skinny child push me around from the start, I'll never get her to do what I tell her.

"Look, Londyn," I say for the tenth time. "You said you wanted Cheerios. I poured you Cheerios. I put milk on the Cheerios. So eat the dang Cheerios."

Londyn pushes her lips into a thin line. I've seen that stubborn face before. On me.

"I already *told* you, they're not the right kind," she says again.

"So? Eat 'em anyway."

"I don't like those Cheerios. They're plain and yucky. I only like the honey-nut kind."

My jaw's starting to clench, but I don't want her to know that. It's an effort to keep my face smooth, but I manage. "Put sugar on it. You can eat grass if it's got sugar on it." I set a plastic sugar bowl in front of her, but she just shakes her head.

"Don't want to." She pulls her arms across her chest and frowns so deeply you'd think she was gonna die if she took one single bite. Maybe that Mrs. Nichols was a fresh, happy woman before she got stuck tending this kid.

I decide maybe I should get down on her level, eye to eye. I straddle a chair and rest my chin in my hands, all the while keeping her locked in my gaze. Closer up, I notice the skin on Londyn's face is puffy, but her eyes have a look I'd missed before. They're stubborn. If I have to watch her all summer, then I know I have to win this battle. It's important that I set the tone.

I nudge the bowl in her direction, right across that plain Formica. "Eat," I command.

Pushing the bowl toward me, she says, "You eat it."

"I don't do breakfast." I push it back.

"Then I don't either."

This is getting me nowhere, so I say, "Okay. Fine. I'll make a deal with you. I'll eat plain Cheerios, and you eat plain Cheerios. We'll both eat *plain* Cheerios. Then it will be fair, okay?"

"Okay."

Muttering under my breath, I get up and stomp to the cupboard and pull out one of those plastic Tupperware bowls. This one is powdery blue, and there's a tomato stain in the bottom. I hate plastic bowls. My dad says it's uncivilized to eat out of anything but ceramic or porcelain, so we've got really nice china that we use, even for breakfast. But while I'm thinking about it I know what kind of dish I use doesn't matter. What matters is that my sister and I are going to get to know each other, even if it kills me. Or her.

I'm getting ready to pour the plain Cheerios into the bowl when suddenly I feel Londyn right beside me. "Wait!" she squeals.

"What?"

She's reaching up into the cupboard, stretching way up on tiptoe, and now she's pulling down the Honey Nut box.

"Now you can eat my plain Cheerios, and I'll eat these," she tells me. In a flash she's poured it into the blue plastic bowl and dumped milk on top. Now she trots over and sits back down at the table, grinning at me. "We can have breakfast now," she says.

She takes a bite, munching so loud it sounds as if she's eating a bowl of raw carrots, and through her bulging cheeks she still manages a smile.

I guess I was wrong about Londyn. She's not dumb. And she's a lot like me.

Which means this could very well be the longest summer of my life.

nine

The dishes are done, I've combed as many knots out of Londyn's hair as either one of us can stand, I've made her brush her teeth and waited outside her room while she got on a faded pink shirt and knit pants with roses on them. She's ready, and I'm ready. Now I'm staring at a problem that I've been trying not to think about: What am I going to do for the rest of the day with an eight-year-old kid?

"Let's watch TV," Londyn says, sensing my thoughts. "Mrs. Nichols liked to watch *The Price Is Right*. How about that?"

"Oh. Well. I'm not into game shows," I say. When she looks at me blankly, I say, "Hey, Londyn, I know! How about a movie! Would you like that? Do you have a VCR?"

"Umm humm," she nods.

Now we're getting somewhere, I tell myself.

"'Cept it's broken."

"Oh."

"But our TV still works good! We can watch *The Price Is Right*."

"But I don't want to watch *The Price Is Right*," I say again. I look at the television, a big clunky set in front of a beat-up copper-colored couch. "Just a second," I say. "Do you get cable?" Even before the words are out of my mouth, I guess the answer.

Londyn shakes her head no, just like I thought she would.

Okay, I say to myself. No TV, and no VCR. It's not time to panic, but it *is* time to worry.

"So, what do you want to do?" she asks me. Londyn's twisting a piece of hair around her finger and putting it in her mouth. Another habit I'm gonna have to break. "Londyn," I say sharply. "Take that hair out of your mouth. Sucking on it is gross."

Instantly, the finger comes out, and the hair unwinds in a gentle, wet curl.

"That's better," I say, more softly this time. I smile, and she smiles right back, which is good because that means she can take it. I wouldn't want some whiny kid for a sister.

"So what do you want to *do?*"

Let me think a second. "Wait—do you know how to Rollerblade?"

She shakes her head. "I can roller *skate*. Except my skates are too little and they squeeze my toes."

I'm about to say "buy some new ones," but I stop myself. Londyn must have read what I was thinking again, because, even though I don't say a word, she answers me.

"Mom says we're poor and poor people don't get everything they want."

I nod like I know what she means.

"Mom says life's not fair and that's just the way it is," Londyn goes on. She sighs and drops into the couch; a cloud of dust filters into the air.

Right away, I hear Londyn start to wheeze. With her free hand she rubs a knuckle underneath her nose. What the heck is my mom thinking, letting the place get dusty when Londyn is allergic? In fact, when I look around the place, I start to consider that my mom's not really on top of some things. I mean, I know she's busy, but there's a bunch of dead leaves curled underneath her potted plants, an empty box of Fiddle Faddle lying on its side on the coffee table, and a stack of old magazines that's got to be at least two feet thick piled right by a chair. I know staying in this much clutter's going to drive me crazy, but I don't want to spend the day cleaning her house. Then I get an idea.

"Hey, Londyn, I thought I saw a strip mall about two blocks from here. Do you know where it is?"

"Sure do," she says. "It's super close, but Mrs. Nichols wouldn't ever take me there. She said walking made her ankles hurt."

"How about if we go there, right now?" I ask. "I've got a little money on me, and I bet we could find something for you."

"You mean, you want to buy me a *present?*" Londyn's eyes get big and wide. She colors with pleasure, and I feel a pang of guilt, because I'm not thinking of buying something for Londyn just to be nice. I'm thinking that if I drop a few bucks at a store it might give us something to do for a couple of hours. But whatever my motives, Londyn doesn't seem to care. She's out the door before I even have a chance to turn off the living room lights.

For the next week Londyn and I head down to the strip mall just about every day. There's all kinds of things to look at, and I can tell that Londyn had never had the chance to buy much. One thing surprises me: it's turned out to be more fun than I thought it would.

That first day I bought her a Barbie doll from the Save Mart. I'd had thirty-five dollars in my pocket and the Barbie was only nine ninety-nine, so I'd decided what the heck, I'll get her the Barbie car, too. I thought Londyn's face might split in two, her smile was that big, and she'd said thank you, thank you, thank you so much I'd finally told her to stop or I'd take everything back. She'd shut up, but kept on grinning. And even though the plastic Save Mart bag practically scraped the ground, she'd insisted on carrying it herself the whole walk home.

"T. J., you shouldn't spend your money on Londyn," my mom had said when she'd spied Londyn and the Barbie stuff. My little sister was doing the same thing she'd been doing all day: shooting the Barbie car, with Barbie inside and blonde hair flying, straight into my feet. I'd stop reading just long enough to kick it back.

"Why not?"

My mom had planted herself between me and Londyn. "Because, it's just not—right."

"I don't have to give Barbie back, do I?" Londyn had pleaded. She'd looked scared. "I don't want to take her back. She's a present from my brother."

Leaning around my mom, so I was talking directly to Londyn, I'd said, "Heck no. You keep Barbie *and* her Corvette. They're a gift."

"Those toys cost a lot of money, T. J.—"

"Not to me," I'd said. Then I told my mom that I'd never had anyone to spoil before, and how much I liked it and that it was no big deal about the money 'cause I had plenty. And I finished with the fact that there was no way I was taking it back, that Londyn and I were having fun and that was that.

My mom had looked from me to Londyn, back to me, and all the while Londyn had been crying, "Please, Mommy! Please! Please? Don't take Barbie. T. J., don't let her take Barbie back!"

"All right, *all right!*" my mom had cried. "Londyn, you can keep the Barbie."

Londyn had clapped her hands, plucked Barbie out of the car, and hugged it into her chest.

"But that's it, T. J.," she'd warned, slicing the air with her hand. "No more presents." For the first time, my mom looked her age. The skin between her eyebrows folded, and shadows had smudged her eyes. "Promise me you won't do it again. I already owe *you* money for today's baby-sitting, and here you go spending more than you earned."

"Forget paying me. I don't want your money."

"What? No, T. J., I insist—"

But I'd shaken my head in a way that made her know I was serious. Why should I get paid when she's barely scraping by? Every dollar she'd give me would be one less for her and Londyn, and all I'd do with it is put it in the bank with the rest of my pile or maybe buy another CD. No, I'd told her, I'm not taking any money, and that's final.

Right then, my mom had looked like she might cry, probably because I wasn't doing what she told me to do. That was too bad, because she'd found me when I was too old to boss.

It was my little sister who'd broken the silence. "I've got a nice brother. Can we keep him?" she'd asked.

Then my mom had started to laugh, had just opened up her arms and Londyn ran straight into them and I sort of scooted close enough so that my shoulder touched theirs. I wasn't exactly hugging the two of them, but I wasn't exactly apart, either.

And that was how that first day ended.

So every day now Londyn begs to go back to that store, promising up and down that she won't ask for a single thing, and every day I get suckered into buying her some little thing. We walk along the little shops, peering into the windows and planning what we're going to eat for lunch, Chinese or Mexican or McDonald's. I get a kick out of watching Londyn shop. The way I buy things is completely different: I like to go into a store, get what I need, and then run out. But Londyn loves to stroll inside and let her hands run over all the products crammed on either side of the aisles. Some of the shops are full of junk, like the All A Dollar, and some have some pretty nice stuff, like the Allied Home and Garden, but Londyn can't seem to tell the difference between them; to her, it's all Christmas morning.

Today she's going all crazy over the flowers. We're at Allied, and she's really nuts about all the bright colors and sweet smells. So I start to think about getting my mom some plants for her yard, to try and spruce it up a little, and suddenly that idea grows and starts pushing out everything else in my brain. I picture how much fun it would be to surprise my mom; I picture her face, picture the way me and my money could make her house look, and before I know it, I've got a plan. It wraps itself around me, and I get so excited to start that I can hardly sleep that night.

Another day and I'm ready to go. My mom's barely out of the driveway when I pull a rusty wagon out of the garage and tell Londyn she can ride in it if she wants, but only on the way down because I'll be getting some stuff and I'll need the wagon to haul it back. She lets me pull her the whole trip, squealing every time the sidewalk drops by half an inch, which is about every five feet. The sidewalks around here are gray and buckled, and the top layer is missing so it looks like a bunch of cottage cheese cement. I picture the ones in my neighborhood, which are white and smooth as marble, and it doesn't seem very fair.

Another bump, and I feel the wad of money in my pocket; I'm remembering that fight over the Barbie and thinking about how weird it is that thirty bucks meant close to nothing to me and everything to my little sister. And I'm thinking about how making her happy brings a feeling, kind of like a small streak of light that goes right through my insides and then sort of sticks. Not that I wouldn't like to bean her a couple of times a day, but still, I've never really *done* for someone before.

It feels good.

Allied's garden shop's in back, so I take the wagon straight through the store, and it's making a *swee swee swee* sound as I pull it along. Once I'm in the flower section I start to load it up. Londyn picks out three red rosebushes and a flat of petunias. I set them on top of the garden soil, which I've already placed on the bottom, and squeeze in some hand tools in a space on the side. Then I top the whole thing off with a long-handled shovel, the best one in the store, and a bag of fertilizer plus a box of Ortho Rose Food.

"Can I have these?" Londyn asks. "I want to help, too."

So I get Londyn a pair of garden gloves with blue checkers on them, but I get me a pair of leather ones that can handle the hard work, and then, with the wheel squeaking like crazy, I pull the whole load up to the register.

The man at the checkout counter looks at me like I'm going to sneak out the door without paying. "You and your sister plannin' on buying all that stuff?" he asks.

That's the first time someone's noticed that Londyn and I go together, and it makes me feel good enough not to snap his head off, which I would have even a week ago. I don't say a word, and the man's face changes real quick when he sees the wad of cash I pull out of my pocket. His eyes bulge while his eyebrows shoot into greased hair.

"You know that Toro lawn mower you got in back?" I ask. "The one that's the top of the line?"

He just looks at me and nods.

"I want that delivered to 1945 Blossom Avenue. I need to have it today, because I've got a lawn to mow."

The man's head's still bobbing.

"So if you can't deliver it today, just tell me and I'll go somewhere else."

"I can get it to you, no problem," he says. "That's right down the street. I'll take it there myself."

"Perfect," I say, and smile. Lifting the money out of my hand, the man smiles right back.

I still have twenty-seven dollars and change in my pocket when I step out of the store and into the bright sun. The wagon's making such a racket I'm tempted to go back inside and buy another, but then I figure I've done enough damage for one day and I keep on walking. Londyn stops licking her Kool-Pop long enough to ask, "Where'd you get all that money?"

"The bank."

"You rob it?"

"No. Don't be stupid, Londyn. The money's mine."

She thinks about that for a second, then asks, "Won't your dad get mad when he finds out all your money's gone?"

"There's plenty left, so don't worry about it."

For some reason, Londyn decides to hop along the sidewalk on one foot. Her hair flies out behind her in a thin brown wave, and the Kool-Pop bobs like a pink baton in her hand. "Won't–he–get–mad–when–he–finds–out–you're–spending–so–much–on–mom–and–me?"

"He won't know."

"How–come–he–won't–know?"

"'Cause it's in my account, and what I do with my own money is none of his business." I'm puffing a little now, because the wagon's so heavy. The shovel drops off, and I have to stop to stick it back on the pile of stuff.

The air is hot and dry, and the walk back is uphill. Right now I could sure use a drink. I'd take a lick of Londyn's Kool-Pop, but it's strawberry and that fake strawberry flavor is so sweet it makes me gag.

I go over a big crack and the shovel falls off again. I set it on the wagon a little harder than I need to. The third time it drops I pick it up and slam the stupid thing right against the roses, which wobble and come dangerously close to spilling onto the walkway.

Now I'm scowling, and Londyn gets the hint. She stops hopping and instead trots close beside me. The top of my scalp is starting to burn, and my palm's working on a blister right where the handle digs into my skin. My back and shoulders are ten degrees hotter than they would have been if I'd worn white instead of black. I make a mental note to get some lighter clothes.

"I like the roses," Londyn says, trying to get me to talk, which isn't a good idea because right now I'm not in the mood.

"Umm humm," I grunt.

"Mom's gonna be so happy. She's always wanted a pretty yard."

Silence. Like I said, I'm not in the mood.

"Did you plant roses at your other house?"

"Nope."

"Oh." Londyn looks surprised. "Did you mow your lawn a bunch?"

"Not exactly. I've never done it before."

"Then why did you buy us a lawn mower if you don't know how to do it?" She gives me a look like I'm crazy, which really makes me start to heat up, probably because I've been worrying about the same thing and don't like her saying it out loud.

"Look, I'll just follow the directions," I say through my teeth. It's no big deal. I can read." I give the wagon an extra hard yank.

"Hey, how come you're so grouchy?" Londyn asks.

"I'm not grouchy."

"You're grouchy all right. Your face is all scrunched up and red."

"I'm just hot."

"Well, I'm hot, too. And *I'm* not grouchy."

"Good for you!" I snap. "Must be wonderful to be happy all the time! Why don't you try pulling this thing and see how happy *you* feel."

She considers this about a minute, which is just long enough for me to feel bad. While she's quiet, I'm thinking about how I'm going to have to change the way I act. Her feelings are probably hurt, all because I never think before shooting my mouth off. My dad and I have been sniping at each other for so long that sometimes I forget other people don't talk to each other this way. I'm just getting ready to apologize when she looks at me. The sun's right in her face, so her eyes are squeezed into slits.

"You know what, T. J.," she says. "You're right."

"I am? About what?"

"About me being happy. I *am* happy most of the time now. But I didn't use to be. Not until you came home."

And then, quick as Rafiki, she runs back and puts both hands on the end of the wagon, her elbows bent out at her sides like broken twigs. With a huff she starts pushing the wagon from behind, her head down and her skinny butt sticking in the air. I want to laugh, but I don't, because I can tell she's serious.

"Aren't you gonna go?"

"Sure," I tell her.

Now it's me pulling and Londyn pushing, and all the while I'm up front, smiling, thinking how much easier it is with someone behind me, sharing the load.

ten

The same man who was behind the cash register at Allied brings the new mower to our house, and it hasn't even been an hour since we left the store. His car isn't much, just a tan Chevy with its trunk propped open because the lawnmower's too big to fit.

I see him before he see me. He's parked at the curb, looking at my mom's house like there's got to be some mistake. He squints at the piece of paper in his hand, then back at our house. No one, he seems to be thinking, with a wad of cash in his pocket like that kid had could possibly live in a place like this.

When he finally sees me he cranks down his window. "Hey, there," he calls out. "This your house?"

"Yeah."

"Oh. Well. Okay, then. Let me pull in."

He backs up, then eases his Chevy into our driveway. The car door swings open. When he steps out I see he's got his jeans tucked inside two snake-skinned cowboy boots, silver at the top and dirty gray at the bottom. The toes are as pointed as the corner of a book.

When he gets to where I'm standing, he sticks out his hand for me to shake. Right off I can tell that it's not a handshake like he means it, but like he's trying to be nice to a kid with money.

"Don't know if I introduced myself before. I'm Sam. And I didn't quite catch your name," he begins.

"T. J. And that's my little sister, Londyn."

"Got your mower in my trunk," he tells me, pointing behind him with his thumb.

"I can see that. Thanks."

"So you're going to mow this lawn." After he hitches up his jeans, Sam leans back on his heels and surveys my yard. At first he doesn't say much, just makes little clucking noises in the back of his throat as he walks around, stretching his head back, then squatting low. I know he's leading up to something, but I don't know what, so Londyn and I just wait. Finally, Sam says, "You planning on doin' this whole job yourself, T. J.? Because, I got to tell you, it surely is a mess."

Even though I've been thinking the same thing, I don't like an outsider saying so. I stiffen up and tell him, "It's a little ratty looking, but I can handle it."

"Think so? What I'm lookin' at is a man's job. You're gonna need to rake the grass out of them dead spots and reseed 'em, and cut back those hanging branches. You got a bad case of dandelions, plus you need to weed-wack every edge in this yard." He rubs his hand across the back of his neck. "I run a little lawn business on the side. If you're interested . . ."

"No thanks. I can do it."

"Not alone, you can't."

"I'm not alone," I tell him. "I got my little sister."

And then I hear Londyn say, "Yeah, my brother 'n me do stuff like this all the time. We're gonna have so many flowers around here and they'll be so pretty it'll make you cry."

I try not to smile as Sam shakes his head, then goes to the trunk of his car and pulls out the Toro. "Suit yourself," he tells me.

Mowing a yard is a lot harder than I thought, but I do it, and Londyn's right beside me, picking up rocks and twigs as I go. My rows are wobbly and my arms ache from all the pushing, but when I turn off the mower and survey the grass, I have to admit that it looks a whole lot better than when we started. There's still burn marks that I'll have to fix, but the dandelion heads have been mowed off and that helps a lot.

By three, we've raked up dead leaves and hoed a tiny patch in the front. The sun's beating down so hot that I borrow one of my mom's white T-shirts and put it on, and when that doesn't cool me down enough, I turn on the hose and drench my whole body. I'm starting to burn, but I don't care, because I'm working for the look on my mom's face when she sees what we've done.

"I want to plant the roses," Londyn tells me.

"Can't. I am too beat. We'll have to soak them real good for tonight, and we'll dig the holes tomorrow."

I see the disappointment on her face, so I decide maybe we can plant a few petunias. Londyn and I manage to stick in two whole rows of flowers before my mom drives up.

She's jumping out of the Jeep like she's been shot out of a barrel. "What have you done?" she cries. "I don't *believe* this! This can't be my lawn!"

I feel my cheeks fold up in the biggest grin I've ever grinned as she waltzes and twirls, clutching her hands under her chin as she checks out the grass, the turned-over soil, and the patches of color that lead up to the front door.

"It'll be better when I'm done with the weeding. I'm getting some more plants and stuff, and I—"

"It's—unbelievable," is all she can manage to say.

"Hey, I helped too," Londyn crows.

"Of course you did!" She grabs Londyn and presses a kiss into the top of her head. "You helped your brother. Just look at this. I don't see how you did it when all I've got is that crappy old hand mower. How . . ." The question dies in her throat when she catches sight of the new Toro. I've tucked it into the back of her open garage, but the red paint shines like a big candy apple. "T. J.," she says softly. "What have you done?"

Now Londyn can't take it anymore. "He bought it, Mom," she squeals, bouncing up and down like a rubber ball. "He bought it for *us*."

My mom's looking at me over the top of Londyn's head, and I brace myself, because I know she's going to order me to take it back. "Don't even start," I warn her. "It's my own money, and you needed it and . . ."

"All this for me?" she breathes. An expression of pure joy washes over my mom, and it's worth every drop of sweat that's run out my scalp or snaked down my back. Right now I know that I feel better than I ever have in my whole life. She hesitates just a second before pulling me into her arms, and this time, I don't resist. My mom doesn't seem to mind that I'm wet with perspiration and that I smell bad. She just folds me into herself and I let go.

"Thank you," she says into my hair.

The next day, I'm back to work, and I can't wait to jump in and see just how far I can get before my mom gets home.

This time Londyn and I start out in the cool of the morning, before the sun starts to cook our brains. When the air heats up, Londyn runs in and out with ice water and green grapes and anything else she can think to bring me. Londyn's right: planting flowers is the best. When I sit back onto my heels, I can see the work I've done, can actually look at the difference I've made. Patches of purple and blue and white and scarlet line the walkway all the way down to the sidewalk. I've planted the rosebushes together right in front of the railing, so that when they grow, their blossoms'll cover the ugly rust marks.

The second week flies by, and the third's gone before I know it and we're into August. Soon I realize I'm in a routine: Nancy picks me up after my dad has left for work, and we chatter like magpies the whole way home. Talking like that is something new for me, but there are so many projects going on and Londyn's doing so much stuff that there's always something to say.

"I don't even know what I did without you," she says most every time I get out of that Jeep.

Truth is, I don't know what I ever did without her and Londyn. And I never want to find out.

One day Sam drives by and tells me that I'm doing a great job, says he can't believe what a hard worker I am and if I ever want a job pulling weeds with him, I've got it. One thing's for sure: My dad would have the shock of his life if he saw me now. I've never done much of anything around his house. The truth is, when he'd ask I'd make so much noise that once he told me I was allergic to work and that I'd better start looking for that rich woman I was gonna marry, because someone would have to support a lazy kid like me. I guess I know now that I'm not lazy. There just wasn't a reason before.

The closest I feel to bad is when my dad tries to talk to me; right now, there's not room inside for more than I've got, so I keep him away. When I start to feel bad about lying to him, I tell myself that he lied to me first, and his lie is as big as mine. I'm not really even his son. Every once in a while he mentions to me how much I'm changing, so I just smile and say thanks and move on to my room. I know he's right. I *am* changing. Maybe it's in inches, but I'm not the same as I was before.

Now I'm standing in the corner of the yard, resting my chin

on a rake, looking at what we've done. Londyn's fidgeting beside me. My mom's yard looks like any other yard, which, considering where we started, is really saying something.

"What are you staring at?" Londyn asks me.

"This. I think we're about finished."

"Good. I want to stop 'cause I'm sick of working. So what are we gonna do now?" she asks me. "Let's do something fun. You want to go swimming?"

"No, there are still plenty more jobs to do," I say, dropping the rake. "And you've got to help, 'cause you're my assistant." I grab her and put her in a neck lock and rub the top of her scalp in a noogie.

"Stop it!" she's squeals. "Stop it! *Stop!*"

I let her go, and she smoothes down her hair, which doesn't help much because I really messed it up.

"So what do you want to *do,* T. J.?"

"I have an idea. Except I can't tell you, because you'll squeal to Mom and this has got to be a secret."

Londyn crosses her chest with her pointer finger and looks at me all solemn. "I *promise* not to say one word. You can pull out my eyeballs and stomp on 'em if I do."

She's so funny I decided to tell her even though she'll probably pop before she'll keep a secret.

"I've got big plans, Londyn. I'm gonna fix up the kitchen. I've been thinking about it, and I'm gonna do it."

"Really?"

"Uh huh. Clean it up. Maybe get a refrigerator with an ice maker. If I'm careful, I might be able to find a stove for cheap. The paint on hers is all chipped."

"Plus it's green," Londyn says, making a face. "I hate green."

"The thing is, I've been asking myself, what good is my

money doing in the bank? Mom needs my help. She needs me."

"Wow. She'll like that."

"Yeah, but it's not just for her." I'm looking right at Londyn when I say the next part. "One of the big reasons I want to fix it is for you. I don't like the way you're coughing all the time. We got to get rid of those dust bunnies."

"You know what *I* would love more than anything in the whole world?" She's twirling her hair around her finger, but she doesn't put it in her mouth.

"What?"

"A canopy bed. I want one with white ruffles, and I want a bedspread with black and white cows on it." She's leaning against me, resting her head against my chest and looking up at me with eyes that have to be as big as the eyes on the cow print bedspread she's so hot for.

"Wait a minute. A canopy sounds expensive, Londyn."

"I guess it is." She sighs a heaving sigh and lets her shoulders droop.

I'm laughing, because I know the little wart thinks I'm a cross between Peter Pan and Santa Claus. I realize she's probably going to get every last thing she wants out of me, and the thing is, I don't care. All her life she's had it pretty rough, so why should I worry if a few bucks of mine make her happy? Still, the canopy's got to be pricey, so I say, "How about we start with that cow bedspread, and then we'll see about the rest."

"Yeah! You are the *best* brother!

Just in case she really thinks so, I grab her and give her another noogie.

The next day I bring a notebook and a pen, so I can get organized about what I should do. I'm sitting at the table with Londyn. She's eating, and I'm trying to plan. Everywhere I look

I see a job; we need a new mailbox. I want a new front door, because this one's peeling like a sunburned back. Plus I make a note to call about getting my mom a new VCR, although I know she'll have a fit if I buy one, and if I did there wouldn't be enough left for the stove I saw in the Sears ad. Stressing about money is new for me. I found out my mom makes seventeen thousand a year, so she's only got pennies after the bills are paid. It makes me feel good to do things for her, and so far, she's letting me. But I don't know how she'll react to the big stuff. I figure I'll deal with it when I have to.

Only one thing right now worries me, and that's my dad. Since I've withdrawn some big money from my account, I can't let my dad get his hands on my bank statement. Lately, he's been telling me he's happy that the dark look has gone from my face and that he never thought he'd live to see the day I wore a color besides black. He says if he'd known a job would make such a difference, he'd have put me to work when I was three.

Night after night I hear my dad come close, hesitate, then drift past my bedroom door. "Good night, son," his voice will call in.

"'Night," I'll answer.

He's keeping his distance, almost like he's afraid that if he makes one wrong move it'll rock the boat. But if he ever sees my bank statement, that boat'd rock plenty. I've been watching the mail, though, and so far, so good.

Now I'm trying to figure out what jobs I should start with first. Except this morning, Londyn seems to be in a mood. She's wiggling everywhere, just like Midget when he needs to go outside. I've already fixed her scrambled eggs with toast and grape jelly, so I know it's not because she's hungry. But she keeps pacing back and forth, her new shoes squeaking on the floor like two mice.

"What's wrong with you?" I finally ask her.

"Nothing. Well, maybe something."

"Then sit down and tell me what it is, or go and watch TV. I can't concentrate with you moving around like that."

She slides into a seat next to me. She doesn't say anything, just stares, which is worse than the pacing.

"Those shoes hurting your feet?"

"Nope."

"Your clothes itching you?"

"Nun uh."

"Then what's up?"

"I don't know," she says. She hesitates, so while I'm waiting I go over an ad that shows new kitchen tables. I'm thinking about how my mom could sure use one of those. When Londyn sees my mind's off on something else, she finally decides to tell me.

"We never go anywhere anymore."

"Sure we do. We go to the store all the time."

"But that's to buy things so we can work. You're always working, and it's—boring."

Carefully, I close the notebook, a little stung because she doesn't appreciate all I'm trying to do. Then I remember she's only eight, so I say, "Okay, Londyn. What do you have in mind?"

"I want to go somewhere."

"Where?"

"Someplace . . ." She runs a fingernail across the metal ring spine of my notebook, and it makes a sound like a zipper being unzipped. I pull it away from her, before she messes up all my papers. Without looking up, she asks, "What's your house like, T. J.?"

"Look around. You tell me."

"No, no, no. I mean your *other* house. The one you wake up in. Is it huge?"

"It's pretty big. But I like this house better."

"How come you like this house better if the other one's more bigger?"

"Because you and Mom are in this one."

"Hmmm." I watch her as she turns this thought over.

"What's your dog like?"

"Midget? I don't know. He's great big. He's a rottweiler, and he sleeps on my bed."

"Can he do any tricks?"

"He burps a lot." And without thinking, I add, "You'll have to come over some time. I bet you'd like him a lot. I bet he'd like *you* a lot too."

Suddenly I know what Londyn's been after. She stops dead still and says, "Okay! Let's go see Midget right now."

"What?"

"Please, T. J.?" she begs. "I want to see where you live at night."

I'm shaking my head, because right away I know that Londyn in my dad's house is a bad idea. "I can't do that, Londyn, no way," I tell her.

"Why not?"

"Because my dad—my *adoptive* dad, doesn't know about you. I mean, he knows I baby-sit you, but he doesn't know *who* you are. And Mom won't like it if we go there."

"I won't tell."

I snort.

"I'm big! I'm almost nine. Don't you think I can keep a secret? Please, T. J., I want to see your house. *Please?*"

I can tell I'm not going to get anywhere with her, so I say, "How are we going to get there? It's way too far to walk, and there are no buses that go to my neighborhood." That's probably a lie, but I've never seen one and Londyn won't know the difference.

"Oh," she says. Her face falls, and for a minute I think that settles it. She chews on the tip of her pointer finger, which is better than sucking her hair, so I let it go.

"Maybe . . . maybe Mrs. Nichols would drive us." Even though she's the one who said it, I can tell Londyn doesn't believe for one second Mrs. Nichols would take either one of us anywhere. "Guess not," she sighs. "Wait a minute!" she brightens. "I've got an idea! We can call us a cab. Mom rode a cab to our house once, and they go anywhere!"

That one stops me cold. Who'd have thought an eight-year-old would know about a cab?

"Now, wait a second—"

But Londyn's too fired up to listen. "You *said!* You said if I could figure out how to get there we could do it. I did! Come on, T. J., you promised!"

An uneasy feeling's creeping through my insides, but I can't think of a reason why we shouldn't go so I squish it down. I tell myself that taking Londyn to my other house won't hurt anything. We can just pop in, pet Midget and Spike for a minute, and then leave. Maybe I say yes because I can remember pleading with my dad to stop working and play with me. Maybe it's because I'm too tired to think straight. Whatever the reason, I tell her it's okay. So I get out the phone book, pick up the phone, and call a cab, and try not to listen to the feeling that says I'm about to make the biggest mistake of my life.

eleven

First thing out of Londyn's mouth is, "Holy cow, you're rich!"

"We're not rich," I tell her. "We're comfortable. There's a big difference."

"Not to me," she says, her voice soft with awe.

Now that I'm looking at my dad's house through her eyes, I can see what she means. The polished marble floors, the winding staircase trimmed in oak, the high creamy ceilings, and the carpet so thick it soaks up noise like a sponge, all make my dad's place seem pretty rich. Londyn's dark eyes widen as she surveys the house, turning toe to heel in a tight circle.

"This is so cool!"

While she's taking in the house I'm watching her, thinking how much she's changed. First of all, she's filled out. She's not round or anything, but the skin over her face has softened and her arms and legs don't look like they belong on a katydid. She's wearing the denim shorts and vest I bought her, a red and white T-shirt, red sandals, and the whole outfit's topped off with a red bow wound in tinfoil stars. I'm proud, because I know she'd fit in with any of the kids in this neighborhood.

The only thing I haven't got quite down yet is her hair; my mom said I couldn't have it cut and I can't braid to save my soul, so the best I can do is brush it into a ponytail every morning. I can never get it right in the middle of her head, so it always tilts slightly to the right or left. Still, it's better than strings of hair wrapped around her finger and stuck in her mouth.

Now I'm watching that ponytail reach down to her waist as she tilts back and studies the ceiling. "T. J., you've got more money than God Himself," she breathes.

"Don't be stupid," I tell her.

"You do, no lie."

There's nothing I can do to get around it, so I try to set her mind on something else. "Hey, look, here comes Midget." I'm patting my thighs in a rat-a-tat-tat. "Say hello to Londyn, boy."

Midget comes loping down the stairs, but stops perfectly still right at the bottom. He's been trained not to go to strangers, so he's looking at me to tell him what to do.

That grabs her attention. "Oh, hi, Midget. Come here. Come see me!" She carefully holds out her hand for him to lick, and I can tell by the expression of pure joy that she really loves dogs. I give the signal to Midget that it's okay, and now he's sniffing Londyn's fingertips, then her shoes and ankles like he's going to vacuum her up through his nostrils. His nose is always cold; when it touches bare skin she squeals and jumps away. I explain that he must be catching a whiff of Barbie and that he's not particular to dolls. I tell her she'd better watch out, 'cause if she smells like a Barbie doll, Midget just might take a small nibble out of her leg.

Her hand's scratching the top of Midget's head, which looks as big as a watermelon compared to her small fingers. "Does your dog ever . . . bite?"

"Naw," I say. I can tell she only half believes me, so I add, "Well, not girls, anyway. The last two kids Midget ate were boys, so I wouldn't get too worried. Don't think he likes the taste of girls much."

"Ha, ha," Londyn says, breaking out in dimples because she

can tell that I'm kidding. "My brother is *so* funny." And then, as if she's talking to a baby, Londyn coos, "You wouldn't bite me, would you, baby? You're a good boy, aren't you, Midget? Yes, such a *good* doggie." She rubs Midget's back with both hands so hard it makes a wave of fur that almost goes clear down to his tail, which is flipping back and forth at about fifty miles an hour. I'm watching the two of them, feeling good because they're enjoying each other. Now Londyn's looking past me, her face suddenly thoughtful.

"Is that a picture of your other mother?"

She's pointing to a small silver frame, nestled with a lot of knick knacks on our entryway table. I can't believe she spotted that so quickly, and I shake my head, wondering that I ever thought she was dumb.

"Yeah, that's her. You can go ahead and look."

Londyn's over at the table, with Midget right beside her. "She's pretty," Londyn says, gingerly holding the picture in her hands.

"Yeah. She was."

Londyn traces my adopted mom's smile with the tip of her finger, touching her nose, then her eyes. Quietly, so I'm not even sure I'm supposed to hear, she murmurs, "Except our mom's prettier."

I know what Londyn's trying to do, but I can't say anything against the woman in that photograph so I just shrug and wait for her to put it back down.

And then I hear a high kind of whistling sound, like air squeezed through a small tube. It's Londyn. She's crunching her nose with a knuckle, a sure sign her asthma's kicking up.

"Hey, Londyn, you okay?"

"Umm humm."

"Wait a second," I say, irritation pricking at my insides. "Are you allergic to dogs?"

A cough, then a wheeze. "Maybe . . . maybe a little."

Now I'm mad, because it always scares me when Londyn starts gunking up. Since I've cleaned my mom's house up it's been a whole lot better, but neither my mom nor Londyn seem to take any of this seriously. And when it comes to Londyn, I'll do whatever it takes to keep her safe.

I'm really fuming when I say, "Geeze, Londyn, why didn't you say so? Midget, come here *right* now." My dog trots over and sits down lopsided at my feet. I can hear the phlegm start in Londyn, but she's trying to act like nothing's wrong.

"It's not that bad," she coughs.

"Yes it is. You've got to use your head! If you're allergic to dogs, you shouldn't be all over Midget. I mean, you've been *petting* him."

"But I *like* Midget!"

"So? The last thing I need is for you to get sick. Come on, Midget," I say, "I got to get you out of here. I'm going to have to put you out back until your sister's gone." And then to Londyn, I scold, "Next time, tell me if you can't be around something, okay?"

"'Kay," she wheezes.

"You've got to listen to me, Londyn. I'm in charge. You hear me?"

Her lip's starting to tremble because I'm barking at her so much, and that makes me feel terrible. I reach over and I give her ponytail a little pull, which lets her know everything's okay. "Hey—listen," I say, my voice quiet now. "I'm sorry I yelled."

"It's okay."

"I just worry about you."

"I know."

"I've got an idea. You want to go see my room?"

She nods.

Pointing, I tell her it's upstairs, first door on the right, and I'll be there as soon as I get rid of Midget. I'm having to drag my dog by his collar because he's decided he wants to stick around and sniff, which is embarrassing because he's usually more obedient than this. The thing is, I've really slacked off his training, so now he thinks he can get away with anything. Since he's not listening to a word I say, I know my dog is just plain showing off.

"Come *on,* Midget! Heel!" I'm pulling on his collar, but he's got his toes pushed out in front of him in eight daggers. If I'm not careful, he's going to scratch the finish on the tile, and that'll tick off my dad for sure. "Move—your—butt," I grunt.

I hear Londyn's voice float to me from halfway up the steps. "Guess he knows who's in charge. That dog listens *way* good."

"Yeah, almost as good as you do, you little brat."

She gives a half laugh, half wheeze as she disappears from my sight.

It takes a minute to get everything done. After Midget is outside, I notice that his food and water dish are almost empty, so I fill them real quick. The dog is staring at me with big sad eyes that make me feel so guilty I throw a ball for him a couple of times. "Go get it!" I yell, and Midget streaks through the grass and then returns it to me, full of dog slime, begging me to throw it again, which I do. I glance at the watch my mom gave me and I realize I've left Londyn alone for about ten minutes, long enough for her to really poke through all my stuff, so I pat Midget and tell him I have to go. The cab driver will be back in less than an hour, so we don't have a lot of time.

As I walk through the kitchen, past the dining room and then into the foyer, I hear my feet hit the tile in hollow thuds. I'm thinking how flawless the inside of this house looks, like it's a dollhouse made of molded plastic that if you set by a heater you'd swear would melt. Tree shadows mottle the furniture and walls in dark and light beads. Everything that's supposed to shine has been polished bright, every cushion has been plumped and smoothed, every plant watered, and every painting dusted and hung straight by the cleaning crew that comes in once a week. It's all so different from my mother's home, which is still cluttered even though I've been working on it every day.

This place is perfect. Perfect, and, I realize . . . empty. A thought startles me, but I know, even as I'm thinking it, that it's true. I don't belong here anymore.

From the bottom of the stairs I call, "How's it going, Londyn? You into my stuff?"

Silence. Spike's making a holy racket, but Londyn's not saying a word, so I try again.

"Hey, Londyn, what 'ya doing?"

I hear the ticking of the grandfather clock, and the faint sound of Midget's bark from the yard, a plane flying low, more squawks from Spike, but nothing from Londyn. Not a sound. Not a word.

And then, somehow, I know.

Maybe it's because the same blood runs through our veins that I can sense what's happened. It's as if I've suddenly been punched in the gut, like an invisible hand has hit me and my eyes are going to explode from my head. I feel what's happened, same as if I'd stood there and watched.

Now I'm running up the stairs, leaping them three at a time, holding my breath so my legs will pump faster. I don't call her name anymore, I just run. My door is half shut; I smack it with my forearm and burst through, and I'm looking frantically around until I see the bottom of her red sandal.

In a flash I'm beside her. Londyn's crumpled on the ground, her knees bent like broken hangers. Her half-open eyes stare blankly into air. Her bottom lip has turned a deep purple blue; even from three feet away I can tell she's not breathing.

"Londyn!" I scream.

I hunch over and put my ear to her chest, but there's nothing but a dead space. No heartbeat, no movement. She's as limp as an old blanket as I pull her into my lap. Her eyes roll back in her head, and a trickle of spit comes out of her mouth.

"Londyn! Londyn!"

I hear a rattle escape from her lungs, and then a silence that's even worse than that sound. I've seen some emergency shows on TV, so I roll her back down and try to pound on her chest, but I don't know if I'm doing it right and her skin's turning pale gray, and I can hardly see her as the tears stream down my face.

"Come on, Londyn, stay with me. Don't leave me! *Don't!*" Her body flops as I pound on her. It's the only movement she makes.

I've got no choice. For just a second, I press my forehead into hers so her eyes blur into mine. "I'll be right back," I whisper. "Can you hear me? Hang on. Please, Londyn. *Hang on!*"

I have to crawl over her to get to my phone. What's the number? I don't know the number! Think of the number, *now!* I'm screaming inside. And then, somehow, my shaking fingers punch 911 and I hear a woman say, "Emergency."

"This is T. J. Lancaster. I live at 8666 Melbourne and . . . and I think my sister's . . ."

I take a gulp, because I can hardly get the words out.

"Get here before she dies!"

twelve

"I'm sorry, Londyn," I choke. I'm stroking her hair, willing her to breathe.

"Listen, T. J., I want you to stay on the line with me. Don't hang up," the 911 lady commands. "Are you and Londyn alone in the house?"

It's hard for me to speak, to pull myself back into the phone so that I can hear what she's saying. All I can see is Londyn, lying there, wet with sweat and deathly still.

"T. J., is there someone else in the house?"

Somehow I manage to speak. "No. I'm alone."

"How old are you?"

"Twelve."

"My name is Cindy, and you're doing just fine. I want you to stay on the line with me, okay? Is Londyn able to talk?"

"No! She can't even breathe! How could she talk if she can't breathe?"

"These are just a few questions so I can figure out the best way to help your sister. Is she choking?"

"No!"

"Is she sweaty or changing color?"

"Yes—she's all wet and her skin's turning blue and—" I press the phone into my mouth so hard my teeth scrape plastic. "You need to send someone *now!*"

"The ambulance has already left the station and they're on their way. Does Londyn have a heart condition?"

"No—she has asthma!"

"T. J., I want you to listen to me. I'm going to need your help." Her voice is quiet, soothing, and it keeps me focused. "Take a deep breath," she says, "and just let it out."

I take in some air and force it out between my lips, and I realize I'm panting fast and hard and I need to slow down or I'm going to lose it.

"Stay with me now," Cindy says. "How old is Londyn?"

"Eight."

"And she's your sister?"

"Yes."

"Why do you think she's not breathing?"

"Because she has asthma and she's allergic to my dog and now she's just lying on my floor and she's not moving. I didn't know Midget would make her so sick! *I didn't know!*"

"Help is on the way, so just hang on. Right now, you and I are going to take care of your sister."

There's nothing else I can do but push my own fear down so I can be there for Londyn. Squeezing my eyelids hard, I clear my vision and try to clear my brain. I've got to do this.

"T. J., is she breathing at all?"

Londyn's chest is flat and still. Her neck muscles are bulging like the spines on a fan; her skin has turned a horrible gray. I press my ear to her mouth.

"T. J.," she repeats. "Is she breathing?"

"I—I don't think so."

"All right. Remember, I want you to stay on the line with me until the paramedics arrive. First of all, make sure she's lying flat. Remove any pillow from underneath her head."

Londyn's already on the floor, so I smooth her legs down and pull her arms straight. Her skin feels clammy. Come on,

Londyn, I'm praying. Stay with me.

"Now, look in her mouth. Is there any vomit?"

I check. "No."

"That's fine. You're doing great. Now, T. J., I want you to put one hand under her neck and put the other on her forehead."

I do it. "Now what?"

"Tilt her head back."

I move Londyn's head, and her mouth parts.

"I want you to place your ear right by her mouth. Listen carefully, and tell me if she's breathing."

I put my head next to Londyn's lips, but I don't hear anything but the drumming of my own heart.

"T. J., is she breathing?" Cindy asks again.

Was there a sound? I think there was and then no—I can't tell! Panic shoots through me like a wave of summer lightning. "I don't know, I don't know, *I don't know!*" I shout to the phone and Cindy and myself and God.

"Try again. Listen, T. J. See if you can hear her breathe."

This time I think I hear something. The soft puff of air on my cheek, like a kiss, and a whisper of a sound.

"Wait—yes!" I cry. "I think—yes!"

"You're doing great, T. J. They'll be there soon."

And then lights flash through my window like a burst of fireworks and a loud siren wail pierces the air and I'm thinking it's the best sound I have ever heard in all my life. Feet pound up the stairs and I scream something, but I don't know what, and then there are three paramedics rushing around, calling out a code of letters and numbers and putting all kinds of tubes and needles in and down my little sister.

"Is she going to be okay?" I ask again and again, but no one hears me.

"Patient is an eight-year-old female in acute respiratory distress. . . ."

My legs feel like rubber as I press myself into the wall. There's no room for me now.

"Bag her!" Someone shouts, while another orders, "Epinephrine, zero point three milligrams IV *stat!*"

I'm squeezing myself into a corner, trying not to take up any space. The thing is, my mind's gone kind of weird; I can't take my eyes off of Londyn's sandal, and how it jiggles every time they pound on her and how she's painted her toenails pink. When did Londyn paint her toenails?

"I want to go with her," I say to no one in particular.

A policeman in black crosses over to where I'm standing, and I get the feeling that he's the only one who can see me. His hand rests lightly on my shoulder.

"I'm Officer Dave. You must be T. J."

I let my eyes flick across his face before I'm absorbed back into Londyn. A paramedic places some kind of mask with a bag over Londyn's face, squeezing the bag in an even rhythm.

"I want to stay with her. I want to ride with her in the ambulance."

Dave shakes his head. "Your little sister is still very sick. How about if we let them do their job, and you and me can follow along in my squad car?" In a gentle voice, he asks, "T. J., do you know how I can contact your mother? I'll need your dad's number, too."

I give him everything he asks for while I'm watching each move the paramedics make. I don't even think, just answer automatically, my voice like wood.

"Okay, people, on three," a woman paramedic barks. "One, two, *three.*" They lift Londyn onto a gurney and crash out my bedroom door. Dave's got his arm around me, holding me up, and now that they've gone I stand perfectly still, and it's feeling so quiet, like the air after a big rainstorm. Dave doesn't move, and neither do I. And then, from someplace deep inside, I let go of a great heaving sob. Once I start, I can't stop. I'm crying because she could still die. And I'm crying because I don't have to be the only one to save her anymore.

Officer Dave's got a broken shoelace. I know, because that's what I'm staring at while I'm sitting on the waiting room couch, elbows on knees and my hands dangling in between. My mom's already rushed past me on her way into the emergency room. She found out about Londyn from Dave. I wanted to be with my sister, so I waited outside the emergency room door until Officer Dave came back and made me sit with him.

"Your mom's pretty upset," he tells me. "She's on her way."

"I–I was supposed to take care of her . . ." my voice trails off. I shift in my seat, because I've started to sweat against the orange vinyl.

"Your dad's coming, too."

"What? You called my *dad?"*

"Of course I called him." Dave scratches the top of his sand-colored hair. "I thought you said Londyn was your sister, but your dad told me she's just a girl you baby-sit–"

"I said she's *like* a sister. Look, you don't have to stay here with me. I'm okay," I interrupted. Right now, my mind is too tangled up to try to explain things to Dave or anyone.

But Dave just shakes his head. "I'll be here till the social worker shows up," he tells me. "I don't want you facing this alone."

"Thanks," I grunt. Then I settled in to wait.

Ten minutes go by and a nurse with teased hair appears and

tells me that the social worker who would normally stay with me is busy with another patient, and would I mind sitting with Officer Dave until the social worker's free? I don't mind, but I bet Officer Dave does, because I've really closed up. I'm so worried about Londyn I feel my insides twist; when Dave asks me more questions I grunt in reply, and after a while, he stops trying and lets me be.

So it's back to waiting.

The noises, the disks of light reflected on the polished floor, the smell of disinfectant and stale coffee push inside my head. Footsteps pound by me, but I keep my eyes locked on the ground.

"Doctor Nolan, Code Blue, Doctor Serena Nolan, Code Blue," a voice announces over an intercom. Is Code Blue bad? A shudder passes though me when I wonder: Is that Code Blue for Londyn? I shove my hands underneath my armpits because my fingers are so cold, like ten pieces of ice. Why won't somebody tell me what's going on?

"Hey, T. J., you okay?" Dave asks.

"Yeah. I just wish they'd let us know."

"These things take time." He sets down the magazine he's been reading, a worn copy of *Fishing Digest,* and asks, "You want to talk about it?"

I shake my head no. He's young, maybe twenty-five, thin, friendly enough, but there're some parts of me I don't want to share with a stranger.

"Okay, well, if you change your mind, I'm here for you, buddy," he says, and goes back to his reading. I look at my watch. One thirteen. Forty-nine minutes since we arrived at the hospital. A person could be all the way dead in forty-nine minutes.

I start to think about the only time anything died on me,

besides my adopted mom and I was too little when that happened to remember. It was years later—I was five, maybe six—and my dad brought home a chocolate-colored hamster that I named Coco. I really loved that hamster. I loved the way his soft fur warmed my hands and the way his whiskers vibrated against my cheek when I held him close. I loved how his eyes looked like two perfect, shiny black beads. I even loved the tiny pricks his claws made as he crawled up my arm and down my back.

Then one day when I looked in his cage, he was absolutely still. Was he dead? I was afraid to touch Coco, to know for sure. From the top of his cage I started to blow on him, but instead of raising up his head he stayed in a tight ball. I blew harder, until his fur separated to the cream-color down underneath and the wood shavings jumped around him like giant flakes of snow. And then, fingers shaking, I reached inside and picked him up. He was cold and stiff; I just looked at him, turning him in my hands like a stone, and I kept wondering where he went. Did Coco have a soul? Did it go somewhere, or did he just—disappear?

And now, I can't help but ask the same thing about Londyn. What happens if she doesn't pull through? If she dies, where would she go? I know one thing for sure: If God takes her, then I won't talk to Him again, because I don't know how I'll live without my little sister.

Approaching footsteps make my eyes fly open. An Asian woman in a white lab coat hurries toward me, her stethoscope wrapped around her neck like a rubber snake. I look at her, hoping she'll stop and tell me about Londyn, but she keeps her eyes straight ahead. Behind her comes an orderly pushing a wheelchair that holds an old woman bent in a question mark. Nobody stops; nobody sees me.

"This sucks. I'm going to go find out what's going on," I announce.

Dave puts a hand on my knee, stopping me. "Wait, T. J. I bet we're going to hear something soon—"

"No we won't. Those doctors don't even—"

And then I hear a voice call out, *"T. J.!"*

My eyes shoot up. It's my mom. She's hurrying toward me with the biggest smile I've ever seen, and in a flash I'm on my feet, running, and she's hugging me so tight my sides ache. It's all right. Now I know everything's all right.

"Londyn is just fine," she says into my hair. "She made it." My mom's rocking me back and forth. The next three words come out in a whisper. "You saved her."

"No! No! I'm the one who made her sick."

"You did not. Her allergies made her sick." My mom takes a step back, eyeing me hard. She's still in her zoo uniform, and her legs are planted into the floor like an upside-down *Y.* "You listen here. Londyn is allergic to birds. She knows that, but I guess she forgot. Londyn told me she tried to hold Spike, and then she couldn't breathe at all."

"Spike! The *bird* made her sick?" Then my heart leaps. "Londyn's *talking?* She's that good? Can I go see her?"

"Absolutely. T. J, she's fine. They're going to have to keep her here for a day or so, but she's really all right. But—but if you hadn't found her when you did . . ."

Both of us let the statement hang. Now Dave's right beside us, smacking my back, smiling as if Londyn was his kid, too.

"I had a feeling this'd turn out all right. I'm going to grab a cup of coffee before I head on out. How about if I buy you a soda, T. J.? This one's on me."

"Sure," I say, suddenly thirsty. He's about to leave when I stop and reach out my hand. "Thanks," I tell him. "Thanks for waiting with me."

"No problem. Ma'am? How about you? Would you like a drink?" he asks my mom.

"Nothing for me, thanks."

Once he's gone, my mom pulls me back into the sofa, and she's telling me how great Londyn's doing and how this is the worst episode she's ever had, and when the nurse asked Londyn if there was anything she wanted, the first words out of Londyn's mouth were, "I want my brother."

"I need to see her now," I say. I'm trying to get up, but my mom's got her hand clamped on my forearm. I watch her expression change, and I'm thinking that this is the second time I see fear cross her face. The first time was when she came in here, and now I'm wondering if maybe she didn't want to tell me anything bad in front of Dave. Maybe she's going to say something terrible about Londyn . . .

"What is it? What's going on? What's wrong?" I ask.

Her brows crunch together, and she swallows. "T. J., I–I know this might not be the right time, but I have to say this. If I don't tell you now, then maybe I never will."

My insides feel like they're being stung by bees. "Is Londyn–"

"No, no. This isn't about Londyn. It's about . . . me." Her lips tremble when she smiles. "You're my James. I told you I was going to call you James, didn't I?"

"Yeah." I'm afraid of what's she's about to say, but I know I've got to hear.

"T. J., when I was driving to the hospital . . ." She stops, clears her throat, tries again. "When I was driving, all the way here I thought that Londyn might–die. And you know what I kept thinking?"

I can't speak. I just shake my head no.

"I kept thinking that—you're my son." Her hands are shaking as she points to her chest, but her voice is suddenly strong. "I gave you birth. *I* gave you life. It was *me*."

"I know that," I say.

"So all the way here, I was thinking that if I—lost—Londyn, I wouldn't have anybody. I wouldn't have *you*. I'd be all alone."

"No, Mom. That's not true. I'd always be here."

"But it's not the same." She strokes my cheek with her hand, and I don't hear a thing but the sound of her voice, which is now almost, but not quite, a whisper.

"Here's the part I want to tell you. I want you to know that if I had to do it again, I'd never let you go. *Never!* Giving you up was the worst mistake I ever made. If there was any way on earth to get you back, I would. You're my son—"

I don't get the chance to hear the rest of what my mom wants to tell me, because a shadow falls over the two of us. When I look up, I see Dave, still holding a cup of coffee, and beside him I see something that makes my heart stop cold.

I'm looking into the face of my father, and in that instant I realize he's heard enough to put it all together. Nancy's not a secret anymore, and neither is Londyn.

He knows.

thirteen

I don't know if what I'm hearing is real, or if it's just because I'm scared, but everything in the waiting room that made a sound is suddenly hushed. The intercom falls silent. The orderly stops pushing his mop in stringy figure eights. My dad's the only one who still has life.

"What do you think you're doing with my son!"

My heart starts kicking against my windpipe—*thump–bump thump–bump thump–bump*. My mom's hand tightens into my thigh while Officer Dave stands bug-eyed, trying to make some sense of it all.

"D-dad," I stammer, "Dad–I–"

"Quiet, T. J." He won't even look at me, but keeps his eyes glued to my mother's face. I've never seen my dad this way. He's flushed red all the way up to his bald spot. He's positioned himself like a fighter: arms bent, fists clenched, chest puffed up like a balloon. There's a fierceness he's never shown before.

"I want an explanation. I heard what you said. What do you mean calling him *your* son?" He's bearing down on my mom. When I look at her I see the whites showing all the way around her eyes, and I'm thinking how much smaller and younger she looks than my dad.

Now my mom's just shaking her head, like she can't even believe what's happening. "Where do I even begin?" she says softly. "Look, I'm truly sorry you had to hear it this way. Maybe we should start over. I'm Nancy Champion." Standing, my mom tries to give him her hand, but my dad shakes his head, refusing to take it. Her fingers flutter back to her side.

"Oh, well. I guess my name doesn't mean anything to you."

"No. Should it?"

My mom flicks her eyes from Dave back to my father. "I think maybe we should talk in private—"

"Here is fine. I'd like to keep this nice and public." My dad's voice is rising, and I can see people look our way before scurrying on.

Dave finally seems to be working again, so he steps closer and says, "Maybe we better take this someplace else—"

"No!" My dad's finger shoots in the direction of the floor. "Let her say what she has to say *right here.*"

I want to pull my arms over my ears, close my eyes, and just disappear into the couch to get away from this, but the time's come and I've got to help my mom face it. Even though my insides are shaking, I'm on my feet. I put a hand on each of my mom's shoulders. "Listen, Dad—" I try again.

"T. J., get away from that woman!"

That seems to be enough to break whatever hold fear had on my mom. I feel her body square, feel her muscles tighten underneath my arm.

"Don't yell at him. If there is someone to blame here, blame me. I'm the one who found him." A heartbeat later she adds, "Mr. Lancaster, I'm T. J.'s biological mother."

And then, as if something inside him burst and all the steam came out, my father says, "No. No, I don't believe you. It's not . . . possible."

"Look, I realize it's amazing—it's a miracle that I found him the way I did. I work at the zoo, and of course you know how T. J. loves animals."

"I know."

"It seemed like T. J. was at the zoo almost as much as I was."
She laughs a fluttering laugh that dies under my father's gaze.
"So one day—I just started watching him. The way he looked, the
way he moved, and I just . . . knew."

"It's true, Dad," I echo. And then, because there's nothing else
to say, I say it again. "It's true."

Still nothing from my dad. He's just staring, like he can't take
it in, so my mom keeps talking. She's all smiles trying to coax my
dad into accepting this, but I'm watching him and I know something my mom doesn't. My dad's like a hurricane; right now
we're in the eye of the storm, and I can tell the other end is going
to hit any minute. I try to squeeze her shoulders, try to warn her
through my fingers to brace herself, but my mom doesn't understand and just keeps chattering.

"Mr. Lancaster, you've done a wonderful job with T. J. I
thank you from the bottom of my heart for giving my son so
much. Over the summer T. J. and I have become very close. Our
relationship as mother and son has been good for us both." She
swallows. "He—he even has a sister."

"A sister?"

"Yes. Londyn, the girl T. J.'s been baby-sitting all summer—
Londyn is his sister. Isn't that . . . wonderful?"

An icy stare from my dad.

"You should see the two of them together. They even look alike."

"Really."

I'm noticing how my dad is all edges: the tie bar that looks
like a blade, the stark line of his collar, and the sharp cut of his
hair. Everything about him looks ready to slice.

My mom's head is bobbing, nodding. "It's amazing, the way
they've taken to each other. She—Londyn—loves him, and I do

too. Mr. Lancaster, I hope you'll try to be happy for T. J. He's found a family."

"Oh? Well, perhaps it escaped your notice that he already has one." And now my dad's ready to speak. Taking a step, so that he's so close now you can smell his breath, he says, "Now you listen to me, Nancy Champion. I don't care who you are. T. J. is *my* son."

"Of course—"

"If he was yours once, he's not anymore."

"But—but I have a right—"

"Right? Right?" In a voice more deadly than before, my dad says, "Your *right* stopped the minute you signed him away."

"Dad!" I cry. "Don't—she's my *mother*—"

"No!" My dad whirls on me. "You had a mother, T. J. Your mother is dead."

The comment hits me across the face. I'm reeling, and he keeps punching, at me and at my mom.

"Listen to me, Ms. Champion. If you even think you can take my son away from me, I'll have you arrested. I'll use every penny I have to stop you, and believe me, I have a lot of pennies. I'm telling you right now that I'm prepared to do whatever it takes." Another breath, and then, "Am I making myself clear?"

The blood drains from my mother's face.

"Good. All right, then. I think we understand each other. T. J., come with me. We're leaving." When I don't move, he shouts, *"Now!"* and I know it'll be worse for my mom if I don't do what he says, so I follow him down the hallway, hating him more with every step I take.

I try not to listen as she cries, "Wait—T. J.! I don't want to lose you!" against the murmur of Dave's voice, and then the wail, "But he's my son! What about Londyn? T. J.! *James!*"

My dad's got my arm now, and he's pulling me toward the

door while my mom's words die out behind me. He won't let me look back.

If my dad's ever been mad at me before, it's nothing compared to the way he is on the ride home.

At first, I try to talk to him. As fast as I can get the words out I tell him how good Nancy's been for me, even tell him about some of the stuff I've done at her house, and then finish up with the fact that my little sister means more to me than I thought anything could and to please try to understand and be happy for me and Nancy and Londyn.

But my dad won't even wait for me to finish before he's screaming, "How could you do this to me?" He says that he's given me everything and that I repay him by stabbing him in the back. "All summer long," he shouts, "I let you go there, thinking you were learning responsibility. You were just learning how to deceive me. You're *my* son, not hers. You'll never go there again, understand?" He slams his hand against the steering wheel and roars, "Answer me, T. J. Did you hear what I said? *Answer me!*"

I don't respond, don't even flinch because by then my insides have turned to stone. I press my forehead into the car window and wish more than anything that I could be out there instead of caged in this car with my father.

Cars, houses, trees, everything's whizzing by in a blur. My dad must be pushing sixty even though we're not on the freeway. His wheels screech as he makes a turn, but I just lean into it like I don't even notice.

"You've shut me out of your life because of *her*. You *will not* see her again!"

But he knows, and I know, that he can't stop me. My dad can't watch me every minute. I'll take a cab, I'll learn to ride the stinking bus, I'll do whatever it takes, but I'm going to be with my sister and my mother. And there's nothing my dad can do about it. I'm not losing my mom and Londyn, I vow. I *won't.*

The car's barely into the driveway before I leap out and run through the garage, up the stairs, and into my room.

"I'm not done with you, T. J.! Get back here!" my dad's yelling after me. "T. J.–*T. J.!*"

Midget sees me and starts racing with me, right by my side, and together we're pounding up the stairs.

"You listen to me—I'm still your father! I'm telling you that you'll never—"

But once I'm in my room I slam the door and crank up my music to drown him out. I look around at what only this morning held all the paramedics and Londyn and me, and it seems as still and lifeless as an empty cocoon. Spike's squawking, Midget's bumping my legs with his tail, and I'm thinking that I should be at the hospital, checking on Londyn instead of stuck here.

Squaaawwkk!

"Just *shut up!*" I demand. Spike's clawing across his perch, puffing his feathers in tiny knives. A pile of droppings mound at the bottom of his cage, showing how much I've ignored him.

I never used to let the gunk pile up. I've always loved Spike, taken great care of him. But since my mom and Londyn, nothing, not even my pets, matters as much to me. When I look at Spike I'm thinking that my bird could have killed my sister.

It's hard for me to know how I feel about that, because everything inside me's all mixed together and I'm so edgy I want to hit something. Before my mom came into my life I just might have. Except I've changed. I know I have to think things through, find a solution, and do what it takes. Just like I did with my mother's yard. There's got to be a way to fix everything that's gone wrong, got to be a way to make it good again. I pick up a pile of newspapers that I use to line Spike's cage and start to work. Fix the problems that are in front of me while I think about the rest.

The newspaper's still in my hand when I hear three loud bangs, and then my dad storms into my room. "You may be finished talking, but I'm not." First thing he does is snap my music off so hard he almost breaks the knob. Then he turns to me.

"I want you to swear to me right now that you'll never see this—*person*—again. Do you swear it?"

I can't answer the way he wants, so I don't say anything at all. My eyes lock onto the newspaper; there is something I see. An answer. A revelation.

"Okay, T. J., play your quiet game. It won't work. One thing's perfectly clear. I've lost control of you. But I'll be dead—do you hear me?—*dead,* before I let that woman waltz in and take you away from me. Look at me when I'm talking to you!"

My focus is locked on the newsprint. A way out, right there in black and white.

"Fine. You won't talk," my dad's words puncture my thoughts. "Well, son, you can still listen. I'm going to nip this thing in the bud. *Nip it in the bud!* I'm sending you away to live with your Aunt Pauline in San Francisco for the rest of the summer and for the new school year."

I blink hard. Now I look at him. "What?"

"That got your attention, didn't it?" He smiles at me like he's won.

"I've just hung up from talking with Pauline. She says she'll be glad to take you in. Let's see how Ms. Champion deals with two thousand miles between the two of you!"

"You're sending me away?"

"I'll fly out to see you, every weekend. But you're *not going to see that woman!* You'll sneak off to be with her the second my back is turned. I won't allow it."

In a way my mind is sharper than it's ever been, like the black print on the paper I'm holding. So he's going to send me away. He's right—that would split my mom and me apart. She's barely scraping by—there's no way she could afford to fly out to see me and I don't know how I could fly back to see her.

My dad has trapped me in a box with only one way out and now I know I'm going to take it. My thoughts are cold and clear because he's left me no other way.

He thinks he's won. But he doesn't know what I know. He hasn't seen what I've seen on the back section of the daily news.

The newspaper headline says: MOTHER WINS CUSTODY BATTLE.

I'm thinking, *why not me?*

Why not get my own lawyer and change back into my mother's son? A judge would have to see that I belong with my *real* mother, that we're blood and my dad's only claim to me is paper. My mind's clicking now. I read the headline again: MOTHER WINS CUSTODY BATTLE.

I could get a chunk of my cash, hire a lawyer, and have him make it legal. Then I could live with my mother and sister forever. My dad could never take me away from my mother again.

". . . *never* let you go. You're my son! T. J., you're *mine!* Do you understand what I'm saying? . . ."

But nothing he says matters now. I've got a real mother. I've got enough money. I look at the newspaper clutched in my hand, and realize I've got something I never had before.

I've got a way.

fourteen

It's been twenty hours since my dad found out about my mom, and I'm looking up at a building that has *Goldfrank, Milewski, and Barr, Attorneys at Law* in big brass letters. No one knows I'm here except maybe the taxi driver, and I didn't say two words to him the whole way here.

"What you want an attorney for, boy? You gonna sue somebody? Did a kid hit you with a skateboard and now you got pain and suffering?" The taxi driver had laughed at his own joke, but when I ignored him he cranked up the radio and ignored me back, which was what I wanted him to do.

Now I'm standing here, wondering what the people inside are going to do when I breeze in and tell them I want a lawyer. The thought's got me frozen; I'm rehearsing what I'm going to say and how I'm going to say it until I can't stand to think it one more time, and then I think it again.

Move! I tell myself. You're ready. Go! Except I can't make my legs walk through those glass doors. I'm just standing there, one hand clutching the newspaper, my backpack slung over my shoulder, while grown-up people dressed in suits bump past me in their hurry to get inside.

The thing is, I'm scared to start this, because I know once it begins it's going to keep going, like an elephant crashing through a forest. It'll crush everything that gets in its path, no matter who or what it is.

The part that pushes me forward is the phone call I made to Londyn just before I left my house. I got right through to her room. When she picked up the phone I knew right away that my mom hadn't told her anything about what happened with me and my dad. "Where *are* you?" she'd wailed. "You need to come see me."

"I'll be there."

"Mom's here. But I want you, too."

"Don't worry. I'm coming soon."

"And guess what? I get to go home tomorrow, and Mom says a cow bedspread came in the mail and she put it on my bed. Mom says you're the best brother in the whole world. I can't wait to go home. I want to see my bedspread so bad!"

"You will," I'd told her, but it was hard to get the words out. "Just—just get better."

Londyn kept asking when I'd come see her at the hospital, said she missed me and I saved her life and mom was all sad and I needed to come fix her, too. Then my mom had taken the phone and said she loved me and Londyn more than anything in the whole world.

"I love you, too, Mom," I'd whispered. I'd never said that to anyone before in my life, and I heard my mother choke back a sob. She told me she'd wait to hear from me and that she's sorry things had turned out like they did. I overheard Londyn in the background yelling, "What things? *What* things?" so my mom whispered that we'd have to talk later. When I told her I love her again, I heard her break down and cry right on the phone.

The sound of her crying's still in my ears, and that's what's giving me courage now. I have to do this. My mother and my sister need me.

I take a breath and I push my way inside. It's cool in here, and quiet. No one's around, which makes me feel a lot better. I don't want people watching me do this.

"Can I help you?" The lady behind the big walnut desk is thin, with a nose as sharp as a bird's beak. She's got the kind of hair that's been colored a too bright red, with nails to match, and when she peers at me I almost turn around and walk away.

"Is there something I can do for you, young man? This is a law office. Are you lost?"

"No." I clear my throat. "I need . . ." my voice fades out. I swallow and say, "I'm here to get myself a lawyer."

Now she's looking amused, which I hate worse than the annoyed look she had only seconds before.

"You need a lawyer? What for?"

I don't want to answer her, want instead to go directly to a lawyer, so I say, "Do I have to tell you?"

"Why—yes. I suppose you do." Her eyebrows are moving up her forehead. "What do you need to see an attorney for?"

I take another breath. I might as well get used to saying it, because I know, after this, I'll be saying it a lot. "It's . . . it's about changing custody. I live with my dad, but I want to live with my mom."

"I see." She clucks in sympathy. "Sweetheart, you can't be the one to hire an attorney. Your mommy will have to do it—"

"She can't. She doesn't have any money."

All of a sudden, she's looking at a stack of papers. In a brisk voice she says, "Then we really can't help you."

I've been dismissed. She's done with me, and I bet she's fig-uring that I'll just slink away with my tail tucked between my legs. But the boldness inside me is growing, right along with my voice. "I already told you, the lawyer isn't for my mother. The lawyer is for me." She's staring at me now, and her mouth goes into a tight red circle.

"Well. I guess you mean business," she says. She's tapping her pencil against the top of her desk. Doesn't say anything, just taps, until she gets something clear in her mind. "Are you aware that a lawyer has to charge for his or her time? Do you have any, what I mean is—"

"You want to know if I can pay, right?"

Now she doesn't seem to know what to say. She's watching me as I lean toward her, bold as brass.

"Don't worry, I've got money," I tell her. I drop my backpack on her desk and flip it open. Then I tilt it long enough for her to see the two thousand dollars I've got inside.

In a flash her face changes, and now she's got a look that I hate more than anything. It's pity. She's feeling sorry for me because to her I'm just a dumb kid who wants a lawyer bad enough to do something this desperate.

She pats the back of my hand lightly and says, "Okay, honey, why don't you have a seat right over there. I'll find someone to see you. And you are . . . ?"

I don't know what she's asking me, so she tries again. "What's your name?"

"Oh. T. J., T. J. Lancaster."

"All right, T. J. Go on, now. Go sit down."

She's on the phone, talking in a hushed voice. I don't know what she's telling the person on the other end of the line, but I'm hardly in my chair before she tells me to follow her. She says she got me an associate lawyer, which I guess means he's new and not too busy to take a kid who just walked in off the street.

I'm back on my feet, following her as she walks down a hallway all the way to the end, and I see paintings of horses and hunting dogs that line the walls in dark green and burgundy. Now she's opening a door and then I'm sitting in a chair facing a lawyer who's probably not more than twenty-four years old. He's got on round glasses with gold-wire frames, a starched white shirt with French cuffs, gold cuff links, red suspenders, and a red and navy striped tie.

He reaches across his desk and gives my hand a firm handshake. "Hi—I'm Steve Povone."

I shrug. I'm too nervous to say much of anything. My heart's pounding in my ears and I'm feeling a little sick.

"So, T. J., Zina tells me you want a lawyer."

"Did she tell you I can pay?" I open my backpack, just like I did for Zina.

"Hold on, T. J. You don't need to prove you've got money—"

I look him right in the eye. "Would you let me in without it?"

Steve doesn't answer. Instead he shakes his head and asks, "How old are you, T. J.?"

"Twelve."

"Twelve. When I was twelve, all I had was a couple bucks in my pocket from picking up aluminum cans. Where did a kid your age get that kind of cash?"

I take a deep breath, and I tell him where. I tell him why I need a lawyer, and why my mom and my sister need me and that they're blood and blood's got to count more than a piece of paper saying I belong to my adopted dad. I've rehearsed it all night, so the words rush out of my mouth like water. He lets me talk, eyeing me from across his desk like he'd never seen the likes of me before. His fingers are woven in a bridge and the tips of his thumbs are resting right against his lips. His brown eyes don't move off me, even for a second.

After the whole story's told I finally stop talking, and then I realize I'm breathing hard. For a moment Steve doesn't say anything. Finally, he leans forward, and I hear his chair squeak. "Well. That's quite a story."

"So are you going to help me?"

"Before we go any further, there's just one point I want to make absolutely clear. Do you realize that an adoption means that legally, you belong to your father—just as if you were born to him?"

"It's the same as buying a pet from a pet store, right?" I snap. "He paid for me, so I'm his."

Steve looks startled. "No—I wouldn't say that, exactly."

"That's how it sounds to me. No one asked me when I was a baby if I wanted to be given away. I was just traded, like some baseball card. Well, I'm asking to be traded back."

With his thumb and forefinger, Steve pushes up his glasses and pinches the bridge of his nose. He's shaking his head softly, almost as if he's got a tremor. "Listen, T. J., this isn't a card game."

"I know that."

"The piece of paper that says you're adopted is for life—"

"You mean like marriage?"

"Well—yes."

I'm ready for that one, because I've already thought it through. "People get married in front of a judge, and it's a piece of paper that makes it legal. Then they get a divorce, and another judge says that piece of paper's no good anymore." I spread out my hands and ask, "So what's the difference? Why's one piece of paper different from another?"

"I—" he stops. I think I got him on that one. "Look," he begins again, "the difference is you're only twelve years old. What you're asking to do, to use your word, is basically divorce your own father." He's pointing at me, but I don't back down. "This will involve a lot of lives. You understand that your father isn't going to give you up without a fight."

"Then we'll have to fight harder."

"Okay," he sighs. His glasses drop back to his nose. "Just say I agree to represent you. There're going to be problems. Lots and lots of problems. For one thing, you're a minor. The law isn't even sure you're a person yet. In a legal sense, that is."

That makes me so mad my mouth dries up. "Listen, I'm a *person*. I *am* a person!"

"Yes—I realize that, but I'm speaking in legal terms—"

I talk right over him, not caring what he thinks of me now, 'cause I'm suddenly fired up. One emotion bubbles over another, and mad is at the top of the pile.

"That is the stupidest thing I've ever heard. It's *stupid!*"

"Whoa, whoa, whoa! Sit back down. Please! All I want you to do is think this thing through before you do something you might regret."

"My dad's going to send me to San Francisco. I need a lawyer."

"All right, T. J." He opens up a brown leather folder and clicks the end of an onyx pen. "I might be able to help you."

"You can?" I can hardly believe what he just said. I'm sinking back into the chair, because all the steam's suddenly gone out of me.

"Yes. I need to discuss this with the partners, but—I think I can take your case. Your mother needs to call my office, and I need proof of your assets. That means you're going to have to have enough money to pay me. More than what's in the backpack."

"I've got $2,356. Is that enough?"

He sighs. "It's a start. How far we can go will depend on your father. Don't kid yourself, T. J. What you want to do is very unusual. However, there have been other cases similar to yours. In fact, if she's truly your biological mother, and she wants custody, then I think we could actually win this thing."

"She's my mother. And she wants me."

Now he's leaning forward on his elbows. "Just be one hundred percent sure you want her."

"T. J., what are you doing here?" my mom cries. She's halfway on her feet when I tell her to sit down for a second, and that we need to talk as soon as I'm done with Londyn. Seeing me makes my mom's face twist in a weird combination of joy and pain, and the expression stays.

"Look, Mom, T. J. got me balloons!" Londyn yells from her hospital bed. "I *love* them better than anything!"

The balloons bat against my head as I tie the bunch of them to Londyn's hospital cart. I try to untangle a knot of ribbon streamers for about ten seconds before I give up, and when I look at Londyn, she's sitting up in bed and smiling at me like a princess.

"Hey, you look great!" I tell her. "What are you doing in bed? You should be home, cleaning up your room." I'd expected her to be all pale, with tubes snaking out of her arms. Instead she's as pink as the balloons, not a tube in sight. It's my mom who looks bad.

"I want to go home. I want to make sure our flowers are okay, 'cause Mrs. Nichols's cats were trying to eat them. Mom, can I have some money? I need to get T. J. a present 'cause he's always doing stuff for us."

"Sure, sweetheart," my mom tells Londyn. Her voice is strained, especially when she adds, "Whatever you want."

I'm busting inside. I want to grab my mom and yell at the top of my lungs that I got a lawyer and everything's going to be okay and no one will be able to take me away, but I need to make sure

Londyn's settled first, so I perch on the end of the bed and ask, "How are you feeling, brat?"

"Fine. The doctors said I can't leave yet because they need to watch me for just a little bit to make sure I stayed okay."

"The doctors told me they're going to give you a personality transplant. I told them to get started right away."

"Oh, ha, ha, ha," Londyn says. She reaches out and grabs my arm. "Are you going to be there when I get home tomorrow?"

"Absolutely," I tell her.

In a flash my mom interrupts with, "Now, T. J., don't go making promises you can't—"

"Don't worry about it, Mom. I'll be there."

Then I reach over and give my little sister a kiss, right on the top of her head, rubbing it in with my hand so she knows I'm not going all soft on her.

"Hey," she squeals. "Stop! Mom, make T. J. stop!"

"No way," I tell Londyn. "I'm giving you a brain massage so you won't be so stupid anymore and you'll stay away from birds."

"Mom!" I'm laughing with her, because she's my little sister and now I know I'm staying with her forever.

"T. J., what on earth has gotten into you?" My mom is right beside me now, so I hop off the bed and tell Londyn I need Mom for a few minutes alone.

"Okay, but hurry! I want to tell you what the nurse said about me."

"I'll bring Mom back real soon," I tell her.

I don't say a word about what I've done until we're sitting at a table. My mom's got a cup of coffee and I've got a Coke, and I watch my mom's spoon stir round and round in her cup, even though she hasn't put any cream or sugar in her coffee. I can tell she's nervous.

"T. J., thanks so much for coming to the hospital. Londyn doesn't know what's happened with your father. I didn't think I should say anything to upset her just yet."

"I'm glad you didn't. She should just worry about getting better."

My mom's biting the edge of her lip. "I wish . . . I wish I knew what to do. I feel so terrible–this whole thing is such a mess."

"It'll be okay," I tell her.

For the first time today, I see a tiny bit of light in my mom's eyes. "What's happened? Did your father change his mind? Will he let me see you?"

"No. He thinks you're trying to steal me away from him. Mom, he says he's going to send me away to San Francisco–"

"What? No. *No!*" She looks like she's been punched. "Oh, T. J.–San Francisco? That's across the country! This is worse than I thought."

I can't take it another second so I blurt, "Wait, Mom, don't cry. I did something just now that will fix it. I just hope . . . I hope you say it's okay. Mom, I got a lawyer."

"A lawyer?" She's pressing a napkin underneath her nose. "You got a lawyer? What for?"

"The only way I can stay with you is if I'm your son again."

"But, your father won't let–"

"I know. That's why I'm divorcing my dad."

My mom's next word is more of a gasp. *"What?"*

"Well–it's like a divorce. The papers saying I belong to him won't count anymore. My lawyer thinks we're gonna win the case. He says I can be yours." And then, a beat later, I add, "If– if you'd like that."

Now I stop breathing, because the next thing she says will decide what my life will be. The one thing I didn't tell Steve was what's been eating at me since I started. My mom's *said* she wishes she'd never given me away. She's *said* she'd like me to be with her. But now, I'm going to find out for sure.

I want her. But does she really want me?

fifteen

My smile is getting bigger by the minute; this time, I don't mind when the cabdriver chatters at me, telling me he's got a kid my age and no way *his* son could run all over blazes like I'm doin', and ain't I the independent type. I just sink into the smooth leather seat and nod every time he pauses for air. I don't hear but every third word he says, because my mind is going over and over what just happened in the hospital cafeteria. I'm feeling like my skin's going to bust from all the joy inside of me, because my mom said yes! *Yes!* She wants me, and we're going to be a family.

At first, when I'd told her what I was doing with Steve Povone, she'd hesitated, and I was afraid it was because she didn't really need me. She'd taken both my hands in hers and said, "I'm sorry, T. J. I can't let you do this."

"Why not?" I'd asked.

"Because it's not . . . right."

"What's not right?" I'd practically shouted. "I want to be with you. And you want me, don't you?"

"Hush, T. J. Of course I do!" She leaned across the table and looked at me, hard. "Now that I really know you, I'm more certain that ever that I should never have let you out of my life. But . . . but . . ."

"But . . . what?" I'd asked, more quietly this time. By then my fear had jumped clear up into my throat. I was so sure she was going to tell me to stay with my dad, that her house was too small, or her life couldn't handle one more kid. Instead she'd squeezed my hands and said, "But, T. J., *I* should be the one to hire a lawyer. *I'm* the one who made the mistake giving you away. *I'm* the one who should pay to get you back . . ."

"You're worried about the *money?* Mom, it's only money—"

"No! T. J., listen to me. That's your college money—your future—and—I," she'd stopped, squeezing her eyelids shut for a moment before she'd gone on. "I can't take that away from you. I thought of getting a lawyer too. It's just . . . I don't have more than a hundred dollars in the bank. There's no way I can fight your father."

"But you're not listening. *I'm* the one who's going to fight!"

"It's just not right for me to stand back and let you drain your bank account—"

That's when I'd stopped her. "Mom, the only thing you need to tell me is if you want me to live with you. If you say no, then I'll tell the lawyer to just forget it."

"It's not that simple—"

"Yes it is. I want to be with you and Londyn. If you want me to be your son again, to be James, just say yes. That's all you've got to say, and I'm doin' it."

Now, as I'm bumping along in the hot cab, I'm hugging my sides, thinking *I did it!* It's like when a snake sheds its skin: The outside of me was sloughed off, and underneath I found James. From now on I'm James, because my whole life is starting over.

". . . well, look at that! You sure do got a nice place, James," the cabbie tells me as he pulls into my dad's driveway.

"It not my house," I answer matter-of-factly. "This is where my dad lives. My home is on Blossom Street."

"Yeah? I've been there. I know right where that is." The cabbie eases up to the end of the driveway, and I'm digging money out of my backpack. While I'm counting bills, the cabbie flings his arm across his seat, twisting so he's looking right at me. He's got short gray hair that's cut so close he looks bald, deep lines in leathered skin, and fingertips stained yellow from nicotine.

"So, this is your daddy's house, and you live way over on Blossom."

"Yep. I'm living with my mom and my sister."

"Mom and sis. Got 'ya." He makes a clicking sound with his mouth. "I want to tell you, James, I've seen this type of thing a lot. See it every single day. We're talkin' divorce, right?"

"It's divorce, all right."

"That's rough." Shaking his head, he says, "Everywhere I go, it's the same thing. Families split apart, then Dad keeps the money while Mom struggles to get by. I've seen lots and lots of breakups, and I'm here to tell you it's always hardest on the children."

He looks puzzled when I grin. I give him an extra ten-dollar tip.

Midget's ninety-pound body is curled on my right foot, and my toes are going numb. "Move, fat boy," I tell him, but my dog only looks at me indignantly before his eyelids flutter back to closed.

"Fine," I tell him. "Just don't expect me to take you on a walk, because my foot's going to fall off any minute. And quit drooling, would 'ya? You're getting my covers wet."

I'm propped on my bed, reading through some newspaper advertisements on outdoor dog runs. The truth is, I've got so many problems to deal with my head feels like it might crack.

I know I've got my biggest problem licked, but a hundred more little ones have cropped up in its place. Like, what am I going to do with Midget now that I'm moving into my mom's house? Londyn's allergic to him. My only thought is that maybe, if he's kept outside, Midget's dog hair might not bother Londyn. But even as I look at the ads, I know putting Midget outside is not much of a solution. My dog's been used to living in the house, and he'll go nuts being stuck behind chain link all day. And even if I get him the best dog run in the world and he likes it, what about Spike? There's no such thing as an outdoor parrot house.

I take a breath and tell myself to take one problem at a time, and the answers will come. So far it's not working. Maybe because my leg hurts.

"Midget, *move!*" I order again. I'm pushing at him with my left foot. Grunting, Midget rolls a whole two inches and I'm trying to shove him even farther when the phone rings, so I'm panting a little when I say, "Hello?"

"T. J.? Hi, honey, it's Aunt Pauline. You sound strange—are you okay?"

"I'm fine. My dog's on my foot, that's all." I hear my voice go flat because I'm not sure how I feel about her right now. The thing is, I don't know whose side she's on, and I don't know what to say to her until I figure that out. It's strange, I'm thinking, the way my world's dividing up. My dad's on one side, and my mom and me and Londyn are on the other. It's like things that are hot or cold, in or out, black or white: They have to be one or the other, because they can't be both.

"So how are you?" she asks again.

"I'm okay, I guess."

"Well, I haven't had a chance to talk to you since your father

called, so I thought I'd better touch base with my soon-to-be
house guest." She waits for me to say something, and I don't
answer. Instead I concentrate on the fur that's on Midget's rump.
There's a little tuft of curly hair mixed in with the straight in a
patch right over his tail.

"I can't tell you how excited I am that you're finally coming
out to my neck of the woods. You—you do know you're going to
stay with me, don't you?"

"Yeah, I know."

"Wonderful!" I hear a puff of air escape into the phone, like
the barest sigh. "So, I was thinking about your visit, and then I
thought, 'Oh, for heaven's sake, Pauline, your guest room is
pink. T. J. won't be able to sleep in a pink room.'" There's a little laugh, followed by a pause. I still won't say anything, so she
keeps going. "That got me on the phone in a hurry. I hired a decorator to totally redo my guest room for you. In fact, that's why
I'm calling. The decorator was just here, and he asked me,
'What does your nephew like? Is he into western things or
whales or the solar system or football or baseball or soccer?' Not
having kids of my own, well, let's just say I didn't have the
faintest idea of what to tell him."

"Hold it," I say. "Just wait a second. Aunt Pauline, are you
having a room *decorated* for me?"

"Yes. The man wants to start work tomorrow."

"Why?"

"You're asking why am I having the room decorated?" she
seems to stumble for words. "Well, I guess I'm having it done
because I want this to be as positive an experience as it can be
for you."

"Positive?" I snort. "Yeah, right."

"Oh, I know it's tough. Look, I understand your father can be a hard man. He and I have had our differences. I wanted him to tell you from the very beginning, but he was too stubborn to listen to anyone but himself."

"So," I say, cautious. "You think he was wrong?"

"Wrong? Of course he was wrong. I don't believe in keeping secrets . . ."

Listening to her, I realize my aunt is on my side. Mentally I move Aunt Pauline into the white column, which means it wouldn't be fair to let her go to all that work when I know what I know.

". . . I realize the circumstances aren't ideal, but I do get to see my sister's child again, and—"

I cut her off with three simple words. "Don't do it."

"What?"

"I said, don't do it. Don't get a decorator, don't paint over the pink. Aunt Pauline, before you spend any money you might as well know that I'm not coming."

"Of course you're coming. I just spoke with your dad this morning and he's already booked your flight."

"I won't be on it." Maybe it's because I'm not afraid to say it anymore, or maybe it's because she said my dad was wrong. Whatever the reason, I decide to come clean and tell her. "Aunt Pauline, I got a lawyer. We're going to court so I can live with my real mom."

"You got a *lawyer?*"

"Yeah. I really did. You can't say anything to my dad because the papers aren't going to be served for a couple of days. My lawyer says I'll be able to stay with my real mom and live with her forever. So, I'm doing it. It's like I'm divorcing my dad."

The third time I said it was the easiest of all. I told the lawyer, I've told my mother, and now I've told my aunt. But instead of saying she understands, her words smack me like an open-handed slap.

"T. J., are you *completely* out of your mind? *Divorce?*"

I take a bite out of my cuticle before I answer. "Yeah. Well, it's *like* a divorce. I want to stay with my mother, and he won't let me. My lawyer's going to get some kind of order so I don't have to go to San Francisco."

"This is *insane*. What about your father! Have you even begun to think what this will do to him?"

"What about me?" I say hotly. "What's he's done to *me?* I mean, you just said that my dad was wrong!"

"Oh, my Lord, T. J., there's wrong, and then there's *wrong!* I can't believe you got an attorney to do this. Did you give the lawyer money? What am I saying, of course you gave him money—" She's starting to talk fast now. Fast, and loud. "T. J., listen to me, you can't do this. Your father may have made some mistakes, but he loves you very much—"

Now I'm getting angry, at my aunt and at myself. I guessed wrong. She's not on my side, so just like that I move her firmly into the black.

"You have to understand that he's scared. There are no rules for this sort of thing. He's trying to do what's best. He's your father—"

"He's *not* my father. I'm adopted. I have a real mother, and I'm not leaving her. I won't."

"Just stop a second and listen to what you're saying . . ."

I don't really hear anymore. I'm looking at the advertisement for the dog run that's still in my hand, and I'm thinking how nothing's ever easy. My plan was to be packed and into my mother's house before my dad even knew what hit him, and now I've told my aunt and from the sound of her voice, she could mess things up for me. Which means I'll have to do things quicker than I thought. I'll have to pack right now.

". . . consequences. T. J.–"

"My name isn't T. J., it's James," I tell her. "I've got to go now. I hope to see you sometime, Aunt Pauline. I'd really like you to meet my mother." And then, just like that, I hang up the phone. I've got to get packing.

sixteen

Packing up my things is really strange. I've pulled out my biggest suitcase, one of a set that my dad bought me for a trip to Disney World when I was six. I throw it on top of my bed, crack it open, and start loading up my life.

Midget's still taking up the bottom half of my bed so there's hardly enough room for the suitcase and all my things, but I figure I'll be leaving him soon so he can do whatever he wants.

I pat the top of his head and start packing. He's watching every move I make. It's like he can tell something's wrong, so his eyes shadow me. Every time I get within range he gives a lick on any part of my skin that's close enough for him to hit, and I don't pass him once without my hand searching the fur on his back. Everything's taking twice as long because I'm petting him. I know this could be our last day together.

My jeans go in, and my T-shirts. Underwear, shoes, socks. Toothpaste, toothbrush, stuff from my bathroom drawers, all the easy parts just fly inside. It's the mementoes crammed into nooks and crannies of my room that are giving me trouble. I mean, what do I do with all the stuff from kindergarten? I'm looking at the clay ashtray I made, painted blue with wobbly stick fish etched on the sides. Three quarters, two paper clips, and a couple of pennies rest in the bottom; I pick up the whole thing and set it next to my flip-flops in my suitcase.

I'll take the ashtray, but leave . . . what? My poster board picture of the solar system? I did that in fourth grade, and I was really proud of the way my planets came out, right to scale. What about my lime green stuffed caterpillar I've hung on to since I can remember? Even though it's hidden in the bottom of my closet, *I* know it's there. It's always been there. So now I'm looking around, trying to decide what to do. I could get some big boxes from our garage, but my shelves full of books couldn't even begin to fit inside, not to mention my science project from fifth grade, or my telescope or my globe. I can tell something about each year of my life by all the stuff.

Just leave it! I tell myself. *If you try to take all this junk, you'll never get inside a taxi.* Besides, my mom's house is too small for me to come barreling in with tons of stuff. I'm not even sure where I'm sleeping; her house only has two bedrooms and she's got one and Londyn's got the other. I shake my head hard, take the ashtray out, and set it back on the shelf.

Everything will have to stay, just like I'll have to go. I'm starting a new life now, with new memories.

With a giant heave, I swing one side of my suitcase up and over, squeeze it down, and snap it shut. And now I'm done. The taxi should be here in ten minutes, which means I timed it just right. So now I'm looking around my room, feeling as empty and jangly as my closet full of hangers.

I drop next to Midget and give him the longest, hardest hug I've ever given him in my life.

"Hey, boy," I whisper. "You're wondering what I'm up to, aren't ya?" My hand's stroking clear down to his paw, and for once I let his tongue work down between all my fingers, something I don't usually stand still for. He's whining softly, and I'm wondering, does he know? Can a dog understand the difference between packing a suitcase for a trip, and packing when your leaving is final?

"I'm sorry I've got to do this to you, Midget," I tell him. "I'll come back when I figure something out. Just don't worry, okay?"

Spike makes a loud noise, so I pull away from Midget and go to my bird, stroking his feathers, which feel like silk to my skin. I tell him to keep working on his vocabulary, because he's really smart and everyone loves a smart bird. He's cocking his head and looking at me, and then I make myself turn away.

There are going to be costs, I'm telling myself, and I have to be willing to pay them. No matter what. I'm thinking I'd better get my suitcase down to the front door so I can leave as soon as the taxi pulls up. Then I hear my door squeak open, and see a dark form fill my doorway.

"T. J.! Where do you think you're going?"

It's my dad.

No! I scream inside my head. No, no, *no!* I'm almost out, almost free, and now this. Right then I decide I hate my Aunt Pauline more than anyone on the face of the earth.

"You're packing? T. J., I don't understand. What is all this?" My dad steps into my room, and I steel myself, ready for the onslaught.

"What are you doing home? Did Aunt Pauline call you?"

"Yes. She said some crazy things, and . . . I told her I didn't believe her. But, son . . ." he stops. I'm watching him age right in front of my eyes. He's looking from my suitcase, to me, back to my suitcase, and his skin turns as gray as his hair.

"Then it's true?" he asks me.

"It's true," I say. My voice sounds bigger than I feel, because I can't leave any room in me for pity. Just think of my mom, focus on her. I know he's going to scream, to yell and turn red and ball his fists tight, but instead he surprises me. He comes over to my bed and sinks next to Midget, and I realize he's all soft and saggy looking. I've never seen him look so old.

"You're leaving me?" he asks. "Just like that?" His voice is so quiet that I'm not even sure what I heard until he says it again, louder this time.

I'm pacing. Back and forth I go, so much twisting inside me I can't stand still. "You know, you're making me do this. I want to be with my real mother and you won't let me!" I'm yelling, because there's a razor cutting through me, and the only way to stop it cold is with anger. Anger kills pain; I've known that all my life. Stay angry, and I can handle this, can handle anything.

"T. J., you can't leave me. You're my son."

"I'm not *your* son! I'm my mother's son. It's her blood in me! Hers and Londyn's. Why are you making this so hard? Come on, Dad, you don't even like me! I'm giving you a break here. I'll leave, and maybe you can get a new kid, one that'll fit you better."

"What?"

"You hate my clothes, hate the way I go to the zoo, hate the way I talk and think. Hate *me!* My mom, and Londyn—they—they like me." I slam my hand into my chest, but I don't even feel it. I can't feel anything now. "No, you know what? They *love* me!"

"You're mine—"

"No! The only thing you got is a piece of paper *saying* I'm yours. You don't own me, Dad, not anymore. I'm not T. J.—I'm James." Now I'm in a rage, pacing, sputtering, doing everything my father's always done when he's been angry. The only movement is when he rubs his hand across his eyes like he might be crying, but I don't want to see. Don't even want to know. Then he looks up at me with the rawest pain I've ever seen.

I can't take it, so I hold up my hands and say, "Look, this isn't doing any good. I'm leaving–"

"Son, will you just listen to me and try to understand? You're mixed up about a lot of things, but none more important than this. The adoption papers didn't make you mine. It's my love for you that made you mine. Mine, and your mother's. The day we brought you home–"

"Don't, Dad," I say. "Just let me go–"

But he won't stop. "The day I brought you home was the happiest day of my life, besides the day I married your mother. Then she left me, and . . . and all I had was my son. And now you . . . you want to leave me too." His voice almost stops, but he takes a ragged breath and goes on. "T. J., I've been wrong about a lot of things. I can see that. But you're dead wrong about what it is to adopt a child."

"It's not the same. Why can't you get that? My mother, and my sister, and me, we share blood . . ."

That's enough to get him on his feet. I'm talking, he's talking, and it's like neither one of us can hear.

"I've had it up to *here* with that blood nonsense. The day I brought you home, you became my child. Not somebody else's child that I would care for, but *mine*–"

"–blood is everything. We belong. We're family. You can't just buy me, like you got me from the store. I decide who I belong to. No one but *me*."

"–I chose you. Other people, your biological mother, didn't want to keep you. *I* did–I *chose*–"

Over the noise I hear a cab honk outside. My dad hears it too. We stop, staring at each other, until I finally say, "Dad, I'm asking you one last time. Will you please, *please* let me see Nancy?"

He's shaking his head, slow and firm. "I'm sorry, T. J. I can't stand by and let it happen. I'll fight her with everything I've got."

The cabbie's honking, and then my dad goes to the window and waves him on before I even know what he's doing.

"Dad, no—that's my cab—"

He turns back to me. "This woman will eat up your whole life and toss me the crumbs."

I make a move to get my things, but now he's got his hand pressed on my suitcase. I can tell he's not going to let me go.

So I turn and run, down the stairs to the hall closet, faster than my dad could even think of moving, and I'm yanking out my Rollerblades. I hear him at the top of the stairs.

"Wait—son! Don't go!"

I don't answer, just strap on my skates, jump to my feet, and head for the door. He's running down each step like fingers fly down piano keys.

"You want to talk about blood, T. J.?" he shouts after me. "You're *my* blood. You hear me? *My heart's blood.* No lawyer, no piece of paper you can get will make that any different."

I skate out the door with his words ringing in my ears.

seventeen

"Well, well, well, look at what the cat dragged in today. I thought maybe you were dead," Marsha says. Her stamp's hovering over the back of my hand, inked and ready to give me the mark. My pass is packed with my things, so Marsha said she'll stamp me for free. Her fake fingernails are painted bright pink. I notice a small gold hoop drilled into the nail of her pointer finger.

"What're you thinking of, starting your visit here this late?" she clucks. "It's already past five, T. J. The zoo's goin' to be closing soon."

"I know what time it is."

She peers through the glass at me. "You look terrible, like you're gonna toss your cookies." The ink rolls across the back of my hand in a black tattoo. "You sick, T. J.?"

"I'm fine. And my name's not T. J. anymore. It's James."

"Ohhh," she nods. "So now you're James. Listen, James, I know what's been going on between you and your momma, and I think it's the best thing in the world, almost like a fairy tale. Nancy is a different woman, thanks to you. Used to be kind of quiet, but now there's not a person around who hasn't heard she's got her son back." She sighs and adds, "Life sure is strange, don't you think? What are the chances of you skating right under your own momma's nose? I guess some things are just meant to be."

"I know," I say, nodding to hurry her along.

"Anyway, it's too bad if you've come to see Nancy, 'cause you won't find her inside. She's still with Londyn. Says she'll be out all the rest of the week."

"I'm here for the animals. So can you give me the stamp already?"

"Well, okay, I was just trying to say hello, is all. You know what I heard?" Marsha says as she clicks the ink pad shut. "I heard you were the one who saved Londyn's life. The buzz around here is that you're a hero."

"I'm no hero," I tell her. "It was my bird that made her sick. Listen, Marsha, I got to go."

"Same cheerful kid, no matter what your name is," she calls after me.

Just inside the gate I drink in the smell of animal dung and heat and popcorn and hot dogs and churros mixed with the sweet scent of suntan lotion. I remember this smell, and I remember the dry, dusty heat that bakes you from the asphalt up. I'm twenty feet down the main walkway and I hear a baby wail from inside the petting pen. A stroller clacks by and a little boy squeals, "Look, Daddy, look at the zebra!" and I'm thinking how I remember this. I remember all of it, like a long-ago dream. I weave through knot after knot of people, moving faster than the rest of them because I want to get away and just find a quiet spot so I can think. I need to think.

Everything inside my head feels scrambled. I don't know where to go. Can't go home to my mom, because my dad'll look for me there and if he finds me he'll make a scene. One thing's for sure, I won't put my mom through that, not until I've got the papers saying that I can stay with her. There's no way I belong at my dad's house anymore. I'm not sure where I should be.

I'm thinking that maybe if I get to a place where everything's in cages, then I can surround my thoughts in separate cages too. Then bring them out, one by one.

I hurry down one side path, then another. There aren't so many people back here, which is why I've gone this way. The zoo is a place I know as well as my own reflection, except it somehow doesn't look the same to me now. All the trees seem smaller; they cast weak patches of shadow instead of the deep shade I remembered. As I walk I see things I never noticed before. The bench on my right is sticky with the remains of a cherry snow cone, and for the first time I notice how shallow the seal pool really is. Sturdy weeds have sprung up between cracks in the asphalt; a little further, and there's a necklace of litter caught against the bottom of the llama fence. Nothing looks good to me here, either, not the way I'd hoped. I thought maybe I could slip back, right where I'd left off. I was hoping at least this place would be the same.

Now I'm wondering, is it me? Is the zoo itself smaller, or am I bigger? And then I stop at the spot I need to be.

"Hey, Rafiki," I say.

Rafiki lets out a screech and swings between silver bars. He's screaming and jumping up and down. I see his sharp white teeth and blue skin on his nose and I know how much I've missed him. I've been so busy with my mother and my sister, I've let everything else in my life just drop.

He's looking at me like he's expecting something. "Sorry, boy," I tell him. When I show him my empty hands, I think I can see disappointment on Rafiki's face. He jumps away from me and settles on a tree limb.

Here I am. I'm at the one place where I thought I'd get answers, but instead, I'm getting more questions. The thoughts I wouldn't face swarm over me like biting flies, and I let them sting because now I have to face everything I've done.

It's blood that makes a family, right? Right! I'm asking myself, telling myself, wishing I could make everything as clear as it was before. I squeeze my fingers into my temples, but I can't make it work. Not now. Because I'm thinking about things from my father's side. I can't get the sound of his voice out of my head.

"You're my *heart's* blood . . . you're mine because I chose you . . . never let you go . . . I love you, son . . ." If my dad is right and adoption's as good as biology, then he *is* my real father. Maybe being there from the start matters even more than whose body I came from. Maybe if I'd done the things for him that I've done for my mom, maybe *we* would have connected too. Maybe some of the distance between us is my fault.

But that's wrong, another voice inside my head argues. Blood is what counts. Blood and genetics—it's what makes me a member of my mom's and Londyn's family, what makes me part of them in a way that no one else can be. We share eyes and hands— she's in me and I'm in Londyn—we're all part of each other. Blood's *everything*. For an instant I think I've worked it out, but then I flash on Philip Champion, my blood father who just disappeared, and I realize he's my blood too and his blood didn't count for much.

Rafiki screams again, and I wait for an answer to crystallize, but nothing comes. What am I expecting to find here? How can a place give me answers if there are no answers? I drift over to a nearby bench and sit on warm wooden slats. There's a pond right in front. I watch as bloated chunks of white bread bob along the surface of the water until a mother duck glides close, gobbling the pieces before her ducklings can reach them, and then I watch as she swims away, leaving a *V* in the wake behind her.

A child's voice cuts into my thoughts. "Daddy," it says, "why doesn't Rafiki have a tail? How come other monkeys have tails and Rafiki doesn't?"

I turn around to see a kid, maybe four, wearing green Oshkosh overalls. Dark hair curls all over his head, and he's holding his dad's hand in a tight grip. The dad is young, maybe twenty-five; he wears tan Dockers and a baseball cap that says Yankees.

"I don't know why he doesn't have a tail," he tells the kid. "That's a real good question."

The dad swings the kid into his arms so he can get a better look, and then they move on. Seems like today, nobody's got the answers.

Six o'clock comes, closing time, and I'm still sitting on the bench when the intercom blares that the gates will be locked and thank you for coming, please visit again. My Rollerblades are stashed underneath the bench. Parents push strollers up the path, a teenage boy's got his arm around a girl with a long blonde braid, a mom in denim shorts pulls twin girls, one in each hand, toward the exit.

So now I have to decide. Where am I going to go? Seems like everyone, everything has a place in this world, except me.

"Hey, kid, zoo's closing," a guard tells me. "Time to go." It's the same guard who yelled at me for feeding Rafiki, but he doesn't recognize me.

"You better get moving, or you're gonna get locked in with all the animals. Gate shuts in ten minutes."

"Yeah, I know. I'm going." I bend down like I'm fixing the lace on my left shoe, but when he's out of sight, I quickly check whether anyone's watching. Then I grab my Rollerblades and slip into a patch of woods behind Rafiki's cage.

There's no place for me to be, so I'll stay here tonight. I'll be safe, because the same walls that keep the animals in keep people out. The further in I go the thicker the trees and brush get. A branch snaps back in my face; my skin's scraped raw, stickers prick straight through my T-shirt, but I don't stop until I'm far enough in that I'm invisible. I pull the vines and underbrush around the bare skin of my legs, covering me until I'm a part of the earth itself. And then, shielding my face with the crook of my arm, I lie back and wait for the darkness. When it comes, I'm still alone.

I jolt awake, and for an instant I don't know where I am; something is crawling on my leg. I smack at it hard before I realize it's just the leaves that I'd pulled over me to keep the chill out, so I tell myself to breathe easy because I'm at the zoo, and there's nothing to be afraid of.

It must be close to morning. The sky's light gray, and the stars are washed pale. Probably close to six A.M.

Right now it's hard to ignore the hunger gnawing my insides. I swallow a couple of times, trying to get as much spit into my stomach as I can to dull the emptiness. Night sounds cover me like a blanket. A bear growls in the distance, something somewhere paws the ground. My back's wet from the dew, and chill seeps all the way through me.

I don't know how much time passes before I hear a sound that almost stops my heart.

Shoes scrape against a walkway, and there are voices. Two, maybe three people are coming my way. Two flashlight beams search the woods, crossing above my head as I scrunch down as quietly as I can, praying that I won't get caught.

"I'm telling you, I would have seen him," a man's voice says.

"I've been walking the grounds all night. All the buildings are locked up—there's no place for him to go."

"But you *did* see him earlier?" a woman asks. I almost gasp out loud, because that's my mom's voice. My mom's here, looking for me.

"Yes, ma'am. Saw him on that bench with his head in his hands, and when I told him it was closing time, he left."

"I knew he'd come here. I was hoping—Lord, where can he be?"

I'm about to run out and tell her I'm here, don't worry—when a second, deeper man's voice says, "If he's not at the zoo, then I have nowhere else to look. He's—gone."

It's my father. My father and my mother are thirty feet away, together, searching the zoo for me. It's too dark to make out more than the barest outlines of their bodies, but I can see them from my hiding place.

A figure that must be the guard steps close and says, "Well, Nancy, if it's okay I'm going to leave you guys here. I've still got rounds to make. You have your key, so just be sure to lock up behind you when you go." A beat later, he adds, "It's going to be okay. I'll just bet he's eating pizza and watching movies with a friend. Kids will be kids."

"Thanks, Barry," my mom tells him.

I watch as one of the flashlight beams bounces away. Now there are just the two shadowed figures. My father is the first one to speak. "What now?" he asks.

"I don't know. We need to think. Do you want to sit down for a minute?" my mom asks.

"No! We don't have time to sit. We need to start looking—maybe he took a bus or the train or maybe even a plane. I should never have left that money in his name. Never. It's given him way too much freedom."

"Maybe it's time to call the police—"

"The police!" my dad shouts. "I don't want them involved in this mess. Not yet. And frankly, that's not your decision to make."

"All right, all right, all *right!* But we need to *talk* about what we're going to do. So let's just take a breath, sit down, and stop yelling at each other, okay?"

She leads my dad to the park bench by the pond. My mom's flashlight shuts off as they sit down with their backs toward me. Inch by inch, I move closer; I'm going slow so I won't make even the tiniest sound. They're talking, but their faces are away from me and I can't make out what they're saying, just the rumble of my dad's baritone cutting in between my mom's soft notes.

I hold my breath and creep closer.

Now I'm behind a small knoll of grass, close enough to make out the words. Dew seeps into my clothes while I crouch, listening, and maybe it's because of the chill or maybe it's because of their words, but I can't stop shivering.

". . . understand?" my dad's saying. "My son is my son."

"He's my son, too. That fact seems to be totally lost on you."

"But you have a daughter, Nancy. I'm alone. There's no one else. You've barged into my life and stolen—"

"Stop. Just stop. We can't start this up again. Let's not argue. We've got to set aside our differences, at least until we find James. We've already lost valuable time screaming at each other when we could have been out here, searching."

"His name is T. J.," my dad snaps.

"He wants to be called James."

Now my dad's voice is rising. "This is exactly the kind of brainwashing I was talking about. You've taken over his mind. That's why I was sure he'd run to you, and that's why I showed up at your door."

"Well, he wasn't there, was he? Which, bottom line, means he's still lost somewhere. And it's dark, and he's alone, and anything could happen to him and—and—I'm . . . so . . . scared." I hear my mom's voice break, and then she starts to sob. "He could be . . . hurt . . . and we wouldn't . . . know."

"Nancy, please. Don't," my dad's voice is soft this time. A flash of white that must be his handkerchief appears and then he hands it to her. "T. J.'s a tough kid. I've always been proud of the way he takes care of himself. He'll be okay."

That surprises me. I never thought anything I did made my dad proud.

Now my mom asks, "But . . . what if he stays away?"

My dad doesn't answer for a full minute, and my mom doesn't press. Finally, my dad says, "That's the thought that has me terrified."

Shaking her head, my mom says, "You must really hate me for what I've done to you."

"Hate? No. Nancy, you gave me my son. What you saw when I met you in the hospital wasn't hate. It was fear. I was—am—*afraid* of you."

"Afraid? But why?"

"Because T. J. is my whole world. You have to realize that I've gone to work, every single day, building a business I'd hoped he would take over. I did it for him, not for me. I've already had my time."

The gray is starting to dissolve into slate blue. The stars have melted to watery points of light. I can see my parents clearly now, my dad sitting to the left of my mom, who's hunched over, hugging her sides. One glance over their shoulders, and they'd see me. I know I should say something, but I don't. It's like I'm hearing them both as people instead of parents.

"Can I ask you something?" A sliver of my mom's face shows as she turns to my dad. "Why doesn't T. J. understand how you feel about him? He always told me . . . oh, maybe I shouldn't," she hesitates, until my father says, "No, go on, I want to know."

"He . . . he always told me that he wasn't good enough for you. I'm not saying it's true, I'm telling you that's how he sees it. He's such a capable young man. He's a hard worker—"

"T. J.?"

"Yes! He's done work you wouldn't believe. Once, he showed up with this clipboard, and he put down all his plans in these neat little rows. He wanted to do things for me. For Londyn." My mom drops her head back, as if she's looking at what's left of the stars. To the sky, she says, "It was my mistake to let him."

"Why do you say that?" My dad's voice is surprisingly gentle.

"Because no matter what kind of charts he makes, he's just a kid. I've been alone for so long now that it was tempting to have someone do things for me. So I just . . . let him. But I'm the adult. I should have been doing those things for myself."

From the way my dad's head is turned, I can tell he's trying to figure her out. I've seen him cock his head that way at me.

"You really love him, don't you?"

"Of course I do. I'm his mother. And . . . you're his father. I guess I haven't really accepted that."

My mom's words stab my gut. It's like I'm frozen, and even though I want to, I can't move. I don't want to hear any more, and at the same time, I'm drinking in every word.

"I've been so afraid of losing him," my dad goes on. "I tried my best, but I guess I was just too old when I started being a father. I'm an old man, Nancy. I'm sixty-two." Now it's my father who's hunched over on the bench, his head in his hands. "I thought if I gave him room he'd come back to me on his own.

Instead, he found you. At least I lost him to someone who loves him as much as I do."

"You did a good job with T. J., Taylor. No, you've done a great job. Kids his age are trying to find their way, that's all."

"But it's taken him away from me."

"He doesn't want to leave you, Taylor. He just wants to be with me. There's a big difference."

My dad's voice wavers, like it's underwater. "Then maybe . . . maybe he should."

"Should . . . what?"

"Maybe he should be with you."

I hear my mom gasp. "Taylor, what are you saying?"

"Just that, if we find him, no—*when* we find him, I should let T. J. live in your house. At least for a while, until he can learn to like me, the way he likes you."

And now I'm on my feet, because I'm free to be with my mother and the fight's over. I'm running, my clothes wet and my legs pumping, and they both turn around and see me and my mother's face is pure joy.

"James!" she cries. "*James!* You are here! I've been so worried—where were you?"

"In the woods, behind Rafiki's cage. I fell asleep."

My mom's loving me up, squeezing me, kissing my eyes, but my dad's holding back. And then I pull away from my mom and stand right in front of my father. My *real* father.

"Dad, I was back there, listening. I—I heard what you said."

He's putting his hand on my head, sort of patting and sort of rubbing my hair with his palm, and I'm staring right into his eyes. Funny how they don't look mean to me now. They just look tired.

"So," he says to me in a drained voice. "Then you know you've got a place to go."

My mom's next to me now, and she's got her arm locked around my shoulders.

"Yeah," I tell him. "I'm going home." My insides are churning, but for the first time in a long time, my mind isn't, because everything is as clear as the water beads hanging off the blades of grass.

My home is with my dad.

eighteen

"Happy birthday, dear James, happy birthday to you," my mom sings, with Londyn and my dad adding uneven harmony. We're standing in front of the monkey cage, and Rafiki gives out a cry that drowns out the last warbly note. I shriek back and toss him a monkey biscuit from the bucket my mom gave to me only minutes before.

When I'd opened the package, I'd just looked at my mom and said, "Monkey biscuits? You bought me a bucket of monkey biscuits?"

She'd told me that since I like to sneak Rafiki food, it might as well be the right kind, and I'd replied that I was pretty sure I was the only kid in the whole world who got a bucket of monkey biscuits for a birthday present. Laughing, she handed me my real gift, a light blue sweatshirt plus some new wheels for my Rollerblades.

Now I send Rafiki a second biscuit, and he snags it in midair. "All right, Rafiki!" I shout.

"That monkey is such a show-off," my mom tells me. "Except he won't do it for me. He never catches anything I throw him."

Just to prove her point, she hurls a biscuit into the cage, where it skitters across the concrete before resting against the back wall. Rafiki just looks at it before he goes back to munching the one I tossed him. "See?" she says.

"Mom, you pitched it six feet away from where he's sitting. A professional baseball player couldn't catch what you threw."

Her lips push out in a pout as she says, "Oh, is that so? You're getting awfully smarty for a kid who's been thirteen for only a couple of hours." Then she grins big so I know it's okay.

The leaves have turned gold and brown; wind sends a handful of them spinning to the ground like paper coins. I've decided October thirteenth is the perfect time to have a birthday, and the zoo is the perfect place to have it in. The air has a snap even though the sun's still trying to warm things up, the animals' coats are thickening for the winter, and best of all, the place isn't overrun with people. Just some moms with a couple of babies in strollers; other than that, it's as if the four of us have the place to ourselves.

But my dad's hanging back, a few feet behind us, enough to show me he doesn't feel easy with my mom and Londyn.

"Hey, Dad, come here," I motion to him. "I want to open your present now."

Slowly, almost as if he's shy, my dad comes over and joins our circle. Watching him, I realize that all of this togetherness is going to take some time for him to get used to. My mom and my dad and Londyn will have to get to know each other at their own pace, which is slower than I'd like, but I remind myself to let things happen however they will. Don't push, I tell myself.

Driving home with him that first morning of my new life, I'd been so tired and hungry that I'd leaned back into the seat and let him tell me why I meant so much to him. And why this would be a new beginning for us. At the end, he'd paused, then said, "I'm glad I had the chance to meet your mother. She's a good person. But now that you're going to be a part of two families, we'll all have to make adjustments. It won't be easy . . ."

I'd forced myself to open my eyes. "But, Dad, they're good adjustments, there's room for everyone."

"I know you believe that, T. J. And I'm willing to try." He pulled down the visor to keep out the glare, and then we were on our own street.

"I—I'd still like to be called James, Dad."

"Why is that?" he'd asked. And he'd looked at me hard. "I thought that business was all settled."

"It is settled. But . . . I'm still part of her. I'm not the same as I was. I'm not T. J. anymore."

He'd rubbed his hand over his chin. After a while he'd said, "I'll never get used to calling you James. You're T. J. to me. But I think I understand. So, *James*, I'll try. Just don't expect too much too soon."

It's worked out that I see my mom and Londyn a couple of times a week, and spend the rest of my time getting to know my dad again, and when my dad asked me what I'd like most for my birthday, I'd told him that I'd like to have a day with the four of us together.

So here we all are, sharing my birthday at the place where I was reborn. And now I feel a hand yanking my sleeve.

"James, guess what?" Londyn says to me. "Yesterday Mom got me an iguana."

"An iguana?"

"Yep. I named her Molly. She's green, and she doesn't bother my allergies one bit 'cause she doesn't have any fur."

Just for fun I decide to bug her. "I'm glad you got a hairless iguana," I say. "Furry iguanas shed way bad. Nothing's worse than iguana hair, because it gets in your food, and then it gets stuck between your teeth and even a toothbrush won't get it out."

"That's not true," she tells me, giving me one of her looks. "There's no such thing as a furry iguana."

"Sure there is. They live up in the North Pole. Santa uses

them to pull his sled when the reindeer are sick."

"Nuh uh," she says.

I thrust my chin out at her. "Nuh *huh*," I say back.

Her hands go on her hips as she wails, "*Mom,* James is being obnoxious again. Make him stop!"

But my mom shakes her head. She's got on worn denims and a baggy gray sweater, and her hair hangs down her back in a loose braid. She hardly looks old enough to be Londyn's mother, let alone mine.

"He's thirteen years old today, Londyn," she says. "I can't make him do anything. Maybe Taylor will have better luck. Taylor, you want to try?"

I'm holding my breath while I wait to see what my dad does. He doesn't like kids much, and he's never really been around Londyn before.

"Well, now, I don't know, Londyn. I've heard about those hairy iguanas," my dad says, sounding stiff as he tries to make a joke. "Hmmm, as I recall, a neighbor of mine once had a pair of green gloves made from genuine iguana fur."

"Nuh *uh,*" she says, but she looks as though she just might believe him, so I grab her and give her a noogie. Her hair sticks up like dandelion fluff. Hearing my dad laugh, I start to think that everything might work out after all.

When I open the present from my dad, he's right beside me, his arm barely brushing mine. "That's the best fishing pole money can buy, son. I bet you'll be out-fishing me in no time."

"Thanks, Dad. It's really great." Now that my mom's taught me how, I reach over to hug my father, and for once, he hugs me back. Then softly, so only the two of us can hear, he says, "I've made too many mistakes. Thanks for giving me another chance."

And I'm thinking how that's true, that we all made mistakes, every one of us. My mom, my dad, and me. Even Londyn.

Rafiki and the other animals are trumpeting their loud jungle noises. I close my eyes, picturing them—Nero the lion, with his heavy mane; Sahib, the old elephant; the jaguars; the cheetahs. Those animals never have to make choices, so they can't make mistakes.

"Maybe we're not perfect, Dad, but we did some things right, too, and that's got to count for something," I tell him. And then, to my whole family, I say, "After all, we're only human."